"Did my brother get you settled in?"

"Brother?"

"Yes. Caleb." She says it like I'm daft.

"I thought—" Of course he wasn't really a valet. "Yes. Thank you."

Rachel glances at her watch. "He owes me a cup of coffee and he was supposed to make a campground run."

"Oh."

"I can still make the campground run if you'll watch the store until I get back." She looks up then, pinning me with piercing blue eyes that match her brother's. I can definitely see the resemblance.

"You want me to watch the store?" I ask. I have absolutely no experience in retail. None. I didn't work through college or any of that. I was a student. Then an attorney. Nothing in between. The only thing I know how to do is attorney-related.

"Yes," she says. "My customers at the campground have been waiting for an hour."

"Okay," I say. I honestly believe that if I refused to help her, she'd send me packing right here on the spot.

I'm getting the feeling that staying in the room Caleb set me up in comes as a package deal.

Help the sister in the store.

Go on a date with the brother.

OUT OF ASHES

A COZY SUSPENSE NOVEL

KATHRYN KALEIGH

Also by Kathryn Kaleigh

The Gravity of Us Series

(Reading Order)

Just Breathe

Just Surface

Just Melt

Standalone Suspense

Out of Ashes

CONTEMPORARY

Alpine Falls (Maybe Yours) Series

(Reading Order)

Still Yours (Maybe)

Yours for Christmas (Maybe)

Forever Yours (Maybe)

(ALPINE FALLS)

Stranded in Alpine Falls

Belonging in Alpine Falls

The Spirit of Christmas in Alpine Falls

Christmas Wishes in Alpine Falls

Finding True North in Alpine Falls

A Ghost of Christmas Magic in Alpine Falls

Secrets and Second Chances

Honeymoon with a Stranger

Not Our Wedding

(SILVER PINES)

The Way Back to You

Back to Where We Began

When We Were Us

(ONCE UPON FOREVER)

My Forever Guy

Our Forever Love

Forever Vows

Finding Forever

Accidentally Forever

(TRUE NORTH)

Borrowed Until Monday

Still Mine

The Moon and the Stars at Christmas

Perfectly Mismatched

On the Way to Forever

A Merry Little Christmas

On the Way Home to Christmas

It was Always You

(UNBREAK MY HEART)

Begin Again

Love Again

Falling Again

(FOR THE LOVE OF THE FLIGHT)

Just Stay

Just Chance

Just Believe

Just Us

Just Once

Just Happened

Just Maybe

Just Pretend

Just Because

(MAGNETIC NORTH)

Second Chance Kisses

Second Chance Secrets

First Time Charm

Three Broken Rules

Second Chance Destiny

Unexpected Vows

(FALLING FOR CHRISTMAS)

The Heart of Christmas

The Magic of Christmas

In a One Horse Open Sleigh

A Secret Royal Christmas

An Old Fashioned Christmas

(CITY SKYLINE BILLIONAIRES)

Billionaire's Unexpected Landing

Billionaire's Accidental Girlfriend

Billionaire's Fallen Angel

Billionaire's Secret Crush

Billionaire's Barefoot Bride

(TRULY, MADLY, DEEPLY)

The Lady in the Red Dress

On the Edge of Chance

Sealed with a Kiss

Kiss Me at Midnight

The Heart Knows

(STOLEN ECHOES)

When Cupid's Arrow Strikes

Chasing Fireflies

A Chance Encounter

(EDGE OF THE HORIZON)

The Forever Equation

Pretend Boyfriend

All our Tomorrows

Kissing for Keeps

Out of the Blue

The Princess and the Playboy

(RED LIPSTICK KISSES)

Red Lipstick Kisses and Small Town Wishes

Stolen Dances and Big City Chances

Chance Connections and Upside Down Plans

A Christmas Kiss on the Twenty-Fifth

Believe in the Magic of Christmas

Vows of Inheritance Series

(Reading Order)

Vow to Protect

Vow to Redeem

ROMANTASY

(IN THE SPIRIT OF LOVE)

Spirits of the Heart

Out of Dreams and Ashes

Etched Upon the Heart

WESTERN ROMANCE

(LONE STAR HEARTS)

Wanted by a Texas Ranger

Saved by a Texas Ranger

(WHISKEY SPRINGS)

Finding Natalie

Promising Samantha

Falling for Allyson

Saving Savannah

Claiming Charlie

Rescuing Keira

Protecting Gabriella

Courting Isabella

TIME TRAVEL

(INTO THE MIST)

Written in the Wind

Scripted in the Stars

Destined in the Twilight

Promised in the Mist

Trapped in the Melody

(DRAGON'S BLOOD)

Dragon's Blood

Lavender Blue

Champagne Silver

Twilight Frost

Mountbatten Pink

(WHEN HEARTSTRINGS BECKON)

Rescued in Time

Meet me in 1879

(WHEN HEARTSTRINGS ECHO)

Messages Across Time

Falling Through to Forever

Once Upon a Winter's Spell

(BECKONED)

Before the Storm

Twist of Fate

When the Stars Align

Once Upon a Christmas

Once in a Blue Moon

A Wish Upon a Star

(BEGUILED)

When Lightning Strikes

Storm of Time

Midnight Storm

When the Moon Falls

Stormborn Angel

(SPELLED)

Time Tempest

The Heart Remembers

A Moment in Time

Moonlight Shadows

HISTORICAL

(TAPESTRY OF BLUE AND GRAY)

Shadows Beneath Magnolia Blooms

Secrets Among Southern Roses

(IT HAPPENED BY ACCIDENT)

Accidentally Alluring

Accidentally Married

(SOUTHERN BELLE CIVIL WAR)

Beyond Enemy Lines

Love Always

Hearts Under Siege

Hearts Under Fire

Away Down South in Dixie

The Reluctant Bride

Stay with Me

Jasmine Kisses

Magnolia Kisses

Gardenia Kisses

(THE QUINNS)

Wait for Me

Take Me Home

Keep Me Safe

FATED MATES

Riley's Mate

Aiden's Mate

Brayden's Mate

STANDALONE SUSPENSE

OUT OF ASHES

ONE

McKenna Monroe

Everything went sideways on a temperate spring Friday night in Houston.

The Houston skyline at night has always has always had a magical quality to it.

Standing on the twenty-first floor of my condo balcony, I'm surrounded by tall buildings. Most of them far taller than my building, but a few smaller buildings scattered here and there.

It's like standing in a forest of buildings instead of trees.

Brightly lit windows. Corporate buildings with people inside still working. Apartments and condos with people relaxing after a day of work. Hotels with people enjoying the city vibes.

I bend down and pull off my high heels, the cold concrete of the balcony beneath my feet. It's worth it to have my feet flat after a long day.

Holding my heels by the straps, I lean over the railing, allowing me to catch a glimpse of the swimming pool several floors below.

Half a dozen people sit around it, no one in the water. Their voices drift upwards, blending with music coming from the concert pianist two floors down who plays beautiful classical music every evening. Tonight is no exception.

I close my eyes and let the music drift through me. Who needs to go to the symphony when there's music like that just outside my door.

The wind flutters the verdant green leaves of the potted ivy sitting on a little table next to my outdoor sofa. It's my only plant. A memento of my grandmother's funeral. I'm not normally a plant person, but I've somehow managed to keep it alive since the funeral going on three years ago.

A firetruck is heading this way now, its siren not out of place, oddly enough.

In the small Texas town where I grew up, the sirens of a firetruck were a big deal. Either something was on fire and the phone lines burned up with gossip about what that something was or maybe there was a parade. Either way, people took note.

Here in Houston, no one pays them much mind.

Firetrucks are routinely called out for just about any emergency. A car wreck. A stuck elevator. A person stabbed on the street.

Living in the city is not for the faint of heart. There are emergencies and incidences constantly. It's just part of everyday life.

When the wind shifts just right, I can smell pizza from the little pizzeria on the street below. Otherwise, the air up here smells like a blend of exhaust, the pungent scent of refineries in the distance, and Texas wind.

Sometimes I catch the scent of the neighbor's two cocker spaniels or the neighbor on the next floor up who cooks a lot of Indian food.

Tonight I don't care.

Tonight I'm happy to be a Houstonian, even if I wasn't born and bred here.

Houston is my city.

And today was a good day at work. Today I did my part to put an arsonist behind bars.

As a criminal prosecutor, I almost always have the public on my side and that's a good feeling.

It's a satisfying job, but it's not my end goal. I want to be a judge. I want to be the person who makes that final decision. The one who weighs all the evidence. Who makes sure the attorneys are playing fair. Who watches out for the juries.

I make a difference now, as an attorney, but it's on a

smaller scale. I hope to make a difference on a larger scale. Later, of course. After I've paid my dues.

Maybe soon if I work hard and keep up my reputation as a good prosecutor. I never say no to a case and I've only lost three cases in my career. It's a really good record.

I won't lie. It's a lot of pressure to keep up that kind of record and a lot of people consider me the one to beat.

When the doorbell rings, I hurry back inside and throw open the door to my best friend. Jennie.

"You're here!" I lock Jennie in a fierce hug. "Come in," I say, grabbing her suitcase and rolling it inside. Lock the door behind us.

"I'm so sorry I'm late. I know we had dinner plans."

I wave her off. "Your flight was late. It's not your fault. How are you?"

"A little tired, but I'm okay." Jennie is a petite blonde with a pretty smile. When she walks into a room, men notice.

I've never been jealous of Jennie. We've been best friends since first grade. She's like a sister to me. I can't think of a single big event in my life where Jennie hasn't been a part of in some way. Good and bad.

Even when I went to law school and she went to archi-tect school, we were there for each other's graduations.

"Want a glass of wine?" I ask. "Or a beer?"

"Wine," she says. "Do you even have beer?"

"I had a six-pack of beer delivered in honor of your visit."

"Then I suppose I'll have a beer then, won't I?"

"Settle in," I say. "I'll get our beer."

"Do I still get the guest room?" she asks.

"I don't even call it the guest room. I call it Jennie's room."

"I'll be right back then. You're still wearing your work clothes."

"I just got home." I wiggle my freshly manicured red-painted toes.

"How do you have time for a pedicures?" she asks. "I swear I'm so busy I don't even think about it."

I open two beer bottles and we go outside to sit on the balcony. Friday night traffic is loud. Teenagers driving along the streets, music spilling from their open windows.

The concert pianist has stopped playing for the night. Too bad.

"It's not like I'm not working when I'm sitting in the salon. You know that."

"Sure. The successful prosecutor has to keep up her image."

"It's not like you sit in a dungeon and work all day."

Jennie winces. "Sometimes it feels like maybe I do."

"How do you like Dubai?" I ask. "What's it like?"

"It's pretty. Clean. But honestly? It's... lonely. People don't socialize like they do here. Or at least not the people I work with. They do their work and they go home."

"How dare they?"

"I know. And most of them are young, too. The

company is strict. We're not allowed to date anyone at work."

"That's probably smart on their part."

"I know." Jennie pulls her shoes off. "It's just there's this guy on my team. Single. And so hot."

"Is he straight?"

"I hope so. Not that it matters. Can't date him. So I barely even talk to him."

"You don't trust yourself around him."

"No. Counselor. I do not. Again. Smoking hot."

"So you're not seeing anyone?"

"Nope." She sweeps a hand down her torso. Like me, she's wearing business attire. A pencil skirt and matching blazer. "All this is just going unappreciated."

I laugh. "Not for long, I'm sure."

"I'm only here for two months tops. Hardly time to meet someone much less get into a relationship."

"Who said anything about a relationship?"

"I missed you so much," Jennie says.

"Me too. You want to have pizza sent up from downstairs?"

"Maybe," she says, sipping her beer. "Actually. You know what I really want to do? Let's go down there and eat. Is that little bar still open?"

"I think it is. We can get pizza, but I don't know about going to the bar."

"Why not? We have to celebrate my being here."

"We do. But with Trevor not being here, it doesn't seem right. For me."

"Where is Trevor Miles these days?"

"He's in Kenya. Working on clean water initiatives in rural communities."

"When you put it like that, it sounds like such important work." She gets up and walks to stand at the railing, looking down over the activity below.

"It is important," I say. "I admire him for what he does."

Turning, she leans against the railing and studies me a moment. "Do you really think he's spending his Friday nights sitting home alone?"

"Well. Yes. Of course." But even as I say the words, I have a sinking feeling in the pit of my stomach. Because do I? Do I really believe that?

Trevor is good-looking. Charming. Outgoing.

Not the kind of guy to sit home alone on a Friday night.

As much as I don't want to admit it, Jennie is right.

Trevor would not be sitting home alone on any night, Friday or otherwise.

Why would he? We haven't seen each other in six months.

Six months.

He calls every week.

We laugh. We talk. We have wonderful conversations about everything and nothing.

But then... nothing from him for the rest of the week.

"I'm busy," I say. "He's busy."

"You're right," Jennie says, but there's a little pout on her lips. "I'm sure you're right."

"Okay," I say. "I'll go out. With you. But not to meet anyone. Not for me."

Jennie's expression brightens.

"Are we going like this? Or putting on go-out clothes?"

"Go out clothes," I say. "If we're going out, let's do it right."

I would rather stay home. I've got some work I could be doing. But it's just one night.

What could it hurt?

CHAPTER
TWO

After sharing a pizza, Jennie and I walk next door to the little local bar.

That's one of the things I love about living downtown. Everything is right here within walking distance.

My own little rendition of New York City. My second choice of a place to live, after Houston, would be New York. I love the idea of not needing a car.

Houston is a driving city and I have a car for running errands and such, but the best days are those days when I just walk to work and back home again. I actually bought my condo downtown for the very reason that it was close to my work.

Jennie and I look good, if I do have to say so myself. We're both wearing solid black sequined cocktail dresses with sweetheart necklines.

But with her blonde hair and blue eyes, she's the one who turns men's heads.

We step into the little bar and find one seat left at the bar.

The music is loud. The conversations are louder.

Not only are all the seats taken, but there are a few people, like me, standing around. Unlike me, they're all holding drinks. Doing the Friday night thing.

What I call the mating ritual. They come here and even though they say they aren't looking for someone to hook up with, almost all of them are. Being an exception myself, I know there are others. There just aren't that many of us.

Jennie walks right up to that empty bar stool and sits down. Does a little flip thing with her hair. I stand back, waiting for a seat to open up.

The next thing I know, the man to her right is up, waving me over to sit on his stool.

"I'm okay, really," I say, walking close enough for him to hear me. "You don't have to get up."

"Anything for my new friend," the man says.

I look at Jennie. She just shrugs with a little smile.

I shake my head.

"What can I get you?" the bartender asks as he slides a cosmopolitan over in front of Jennie.

"Just water with lemon," I say. "How did you get that so fast?" I ask her.

"I have skills."

"Yes. You do. Impressive skills, too."

"Well. You already knew that."

Jennie is in her element. I had forgotten just how much being out like this was her element.

She takes a sip of her pretty pink drink. "You sure you don't want anything?"

"I had that beer."

"Which you barely even touched."

"I have lots of work to do tomorrow. I need a clear head."

"All work and no play..." she says.

"Hush now," I say. "I'm here, aren't I?"

"You are here," she agrees. "Reluctantly as it may be."

"What about your friend?" I ask, looking over my shoulder for the guy who gave up his seat for me. "Shouldn't you be talking to him?"

"Oh." She waves a hand. "I told him I'd find him later."

"I don't see how you do it," I say, picking up my glass of water and taking a sip. "I can see why you're not digging Dubai."

"I know, right?"

"You don't go out by yourself?"

She makes a face. "Not my style. It reeks of desperation."

"You are most certainly not a desperate woman."

"Nope," she says, flipping her hair back. "I'm just a girl who likes to have fun. After working hard, of course."

"Of course. So tell me how you really ended up back here?" I ask.

"Dubai was temporary."

"Oh." I shift on the bar stool, leaning away from a young man who squeezes in on my other side to place a drink order. "I thought you're heading back there. In what? Two months?"

"I don't think it'll be Dubai."

"Where then? And how did you get so lucky to get to travel the world?"

"Berlin maybe. At least that's what they're saying. And not so sure just how lucky I am. If you were with me, it would be different. But I'm not really into traveling the world by myself."

"I get it." I glance around at the people in the bar. People I've never seen before, despite living right above this place. "But this where I belong."

"I know." She puts a hand on my wrist. "I would never ask you to give up your dream of being a judge."

I shift a little uncomfortably. She's the only person who knows that being a judge is my dream. Jennie is the only person who knows a lot of things about me.

Even though we grew up together and shared every single thought with each other, I'm not really that person anymore. I'm creating a new life for myself.

A life where I'm a serious prosecutor not a giggling girl who shares everything with her best friend.

"Of course," I say. "I'm just going to find the restroom. Don't run off with anyone, okay?"

"I promise I will be right here when you get back. And I'll save your seat."

"Don't make promises you can't keep," I say before I start the process of weaving my way through the bar toward the restroom.

Once inside the restroom, I take a breath.

The noise level is several decibels lower in here than it was in the main part of the bar.

I can actually hear myself think.

Sitting on a stool in front of a gilded mirror, I refresh my lip gloss.

Two girls, giggling and obviously a little drunk walk around me like I'm not even there.

Bars have never really been my scene. Anytime I went, it was because Jennie wanted to go.

It was often entertaining. Mostly watching her talk to men. Get their hopes up. Then leave with me. Not saying she didn't get more than a few numbers and I'm pretty sure she even called a few of them.

I got a few numbers myself, but I never called them. I prefer to meet my guys the safe way. On the Internet. That way I have time to vet them properly before spending any actual time getting to know them.

It's worked well so far.

Just because my current boyfriend is halfway across the world has nothing to do with it.

I rather like it that way. It gives me more time to focus on my career.

I always feel like my life will be better if I can just get to the next level of my career.

I'm not even sure where I got that from. I didn't get it from my mother. She was content to stay home take care of the house. I didn't get it from my father. He was content to just work. Earn his pay and go home.

And they're doing what all successfully retired parents do. They're traveling.

I'm the only person in my life who isn't traveling.

I don't even like traveling.

There are airline schedules. Hotels. Rental cars.

In my experience, there is nothing fun about spending the night in a strange place. Worrying about checkout times. Where to get coffee and breakfast.

Where to get anything.

I like my routine. My home. My schedule.

I like knowing what I'm going to do and where I'm going to be from one day to the next.

It's okay to not like travel.

Just because everyone else is doing it doesn't mean I have to do it.

I glance at the time on my phone and wonder how much longer before I can convince Jennie that it's time to go home.

Heading back toward our seats at the bar, a sense of panic sweeps over me.

Jennie isn't where I left here. Two other people are sitting in our seats. I wasn't gone THAT long. She promised she wouldn't leave without me.

Headlines flash through my head.

Young lady last seen at bar. Never seen again.

Then I see her on the dance floor with her new friend along with a dozen other people crowded into the little dance area.

Relief washes through me.

I'm such an overprotective friend. But then in my work, my focus is on sending people who hurt people like Jennie to prison.

It's just my everyday world.

It's like the firetrucks that no one notices.

But I notice.

It's my world.

CHAPTER

THREE

I'm good at making the best of wherever I am.

I wrangle my way up to the bar and order myself a fresh sparkling water with lime.

Then I find an empty chair to sit in while I wait for Jennie to close the place down.

As much as I'm ready to go home, I know how she is. She'll close the place down. And being the good friend that I am, I won't leave her alone. Too many things could go awry.

She's still dancing with the same guy. That's not so unusual.

As I sit there, with the loud music spilling over me, I reflect on my day.

It was a good day.

I put another person behind bars.

The girl sitting next to me gets up and a minute later, a man sits down next to me.

"Hi," he says. "What's a girl like you doing sitting here by herself?"

"Just waiting for my friend," I say.

"Doesn't sound like a good way to spend a Friday night. Just waiting."

"I have a boyfriend," I say.

"It's okay," he says, holding up his hands. "Just looking for some conversation."

I take a second to study him. He looks like a nice enough guy. The kind of guy I work with. He could even be an attorney. But fortunately I don't recognize him. I don't care to be spotted hanging out in a bar, even if I am just drinking sparkling water.

I've got my reputation to protect. The one my future judge-seeking self will appreciate one day.

"Okay," I say. "Tell me about you."

"I'm Adam and I'm in a band."

I look at him again and try to keep a straight face.

"You don't look like the kind of guy who's in a band," I say.

"It's my night off."

I think about the concert pianist. I've never known him

to miss a night. Unless he's in a concert. Musicians don't take days off.

But I decide not to confront him.

At least not directly.

"Okay Adam. What's your day job?"

He looks crestfallen. Like I've just seen straight through his game.

"I'm an accountant," he says.

I nod. "You look like an accountant."

"Well then," he says. "I'll have to work on that, won't I?"

"Yes—" I glance in Jennie's direction. My job, after all, is to make sure she doesn't become one of those girls who goes missing and is never seen again.

But it's not Jennie that catches my attention. It's the man sitting alone behind her.

In just that one instant, recognition slides along my spine and somehow settles like a bur in the back of my throat.

I know that man.

I spent days looking at his face across a courtroom. And that was after days of looking at his face in a case file in preparation for that trial.

He wasn't supposed to ever see the outside of a prison.

And what's more. He's watching me. With his bottomless black eyes. I may not can see them across the room, but I spent enough time looking into them that I'll never forget them.

In that instant, I realize that not only did I spend days looking at him, he spent those same days looking at me.

"I'm sorry," I murmur to the man sitting next to me as I pull out my phone. "I have to…"

I stare at the message on my screen.

MILES

You should know. He's out.

There's more to the message, but I don't need to read it. I'll read it later.

I know exactly who he's talking about. He's talking about Silas Crowe.

My most difficult and heaviest case. Silas Crowe killed his girlfriend.

The evidence was irrefutable and I convinced a jury of that. They put him away for life.

Or so it was supposed to be.

But things happen. They happen all the time.

People get out of prison for all sorts of reasons.

Reasons I can't even think about right now. There are too many to name.

As I fist my hands together in my lap, keeping my face expressionless, I force myself to do the math.

Silas Crowe has been in prison for four years. Some days I don't even think about him, at least not much more than in passing.

He'd made my reputation. No one thought it could be done.

But I'd been young and determined. Fearless.

I hadn't thought about the possibility that he might get out of prison.

That he might be sitting across a bar not far from my home, looking at me.

Cold. Calculating.

Even across the room, I see those cold, calculating snake eyes watching me. He looks the way he'd looked in the photos I'd studied. Before the trial. Bearded. Scraggly.

He doesn't belong here. His clothes are wrong, but no one pays him any mind. He's wearing tan pants with a blue shirt. Some kind of uniform. I can't make out the words stitched on his pocket.

How can no one notice that he doesn't belong here? They walk around him like he's a piece of furniture. Old furniture. He's in his mid-thirties, but could easily pass for fifty years old.

There's nothing in his hands. No drink. He's so obviously here for the sole reason of finding me.

He's gotten out and he's tracked me down.

Other than my hands fisting around my phone, I don't move a muscle.

Adam is saying something, but I don't hear him.

I turn to look at him, force a smile onto my face.

"Adam," I say. "How would you like to do a good deed tonight?"

"I'm always up for a good deed," he drawls. "What's in it for me?"

"Knowing you saved a life."

A little dramatic perhaps, but I need his help.

Jennie is between me and Silas Crowe. Approaching Jennie means getting far too close to Silas.

"What's the favor?" Adam asks, still hoping there's something in it for him, no doubt.

"See that girl on the dance floor? The pretty blonde wearing the black dress?"

"I see her."

"Walk up to her. Say *there's an emergency and McKenna needs to leave.*"

"That's it?"

"That's it. Say it back."

"There's an emergency and McKenna needs to leave."

"Now. If she resists, add *now.*"

"You do look kind of pale."

I turn and look in Adam's brown eyes. "Because there's an emergency. This is urgent, Adam. Life or death. Will you help me?"

"Sure. Sure. I'll do it."

"Good. Do it now."

"I got this," Adam says.

Under other circumstances, I might find this amusing. But there is nothing amusing about it right now.

I keep my gaze on Silas Crowe as Adam makes his way over to Jennie.

Adam looks back at me just before he taps Jennie on the shoulder and delivers the message.

Jennie's gaze lands on mine.

Maybe she sees the shock on my face.

She won't know what's wrong, but she doesn't need to know right now.

All she needs to know is that we need to get out of here. Now.

She says something to her friend and dance partner.

He doesn't want to let go of her hand. To her credit, Jennie pulls loose and follows Adam back in my direction.

It occurs to me then that I can't let Silas Crowe see me talking to Jennie.

The thought crashes into my head that I might be too late.

Refusing to accept the possibility, I stand up and whirl around heading back to the restroom. Jennie will know to follow me.

She'll know.

Inside the restroom, after checking to make sure I'm alone, I lean against the wall and wait for Jennie to join me.

"What's wrong?" she asks, coming through the door.

"You don't know me," I say, turning the door lock. "Okay? From here on out, you do not know me."

"Okay." Her brow creases in concern. "What happened?"

Panic gathers in my throat.

"McKenna. Sit down."

I drop onto the vanity chair where I sat earlier.

"There was a case. About four years ago. My first big case. You might remember it. A man killed his girlfriend."

"Of course I remember. It's all you talked about for months."

"It's all I thought about for months." I shove at my hair. Breathe in. Breathe out.

Jennie leans on the counter. Puts a hand on my shoulder. Waits.

Someone tries the doorknob. When it doesn't open, they knock.

"Just a minute," Jennie says.

"He's here," I say, my voice barely more than a whisper.

"Here. Where?"

"Out there. In the bar. Silas Crowe. He... he saw me."

"But how? Didn't he get the death penalty?"

"Yes. I don't know how. I just know he's out there."

Jennie pales and drops onto the edge of the chair next to me.

"Are you sure?"

I hold up my phone where the text message is still front and center.

"You think he found you?"

"Yes." I don't want to think it. I want to think it's random. But it can't be random. It's too much to be random.

I have a very vivid memory of the words Silas Crowe spoke to me as they carried him away after the verdict.

He'd been wearing a light gray suit that was too big for

him. A gaunt man, wasting away in jail. His face clean-shaven, too clean-shaven. So different from his photos. Hollowed out cheeks. Thin lips. Eyes full of hate and evil that he could turn on and off at will.

With the full extent of that evil turn on, he looked right into my eyes as he walked past, hands safely cuffed behind his back. "You'll pay for this." He hissed the words through gapped teeth, spitting them at me like a venomous snake.

I'd felt safe. Stupidly safe. And I'd been so stupidly proud of myself in that moment. Ignoring the chills that he gave me. I'd held me head high and I hadn't looked away.

I'd won.

I'd sent the bad guy away.

But now the bad guy was out of prison and he was here. He'd found me.

"We have to get out of here," I say, hugging my stomach that threatened to roil with the shock of it all.

"Okay. He'll see us leave."

"There will be no us," I say. "He can't see us together."

"What then?"

I have to think. I have to figure this out.

"You leave first. Go straight to my condo. Take your new guy friend if you can."

"Okay."

"I'll call an Uber." My hands shake as I unlock my phone. "Drive around for a minute, then meet you at home."

"It's so cloak and dagger," Jennie says.

"Jennie." I grab her hand. "He's dangerous. He's a dangerous man. Do you understand?"

"Yes. I understand." She stands up. "I'll see you at your condo."

I stand up and hug her. "I love you."

"Love you, too. Now. Let's get out of here."

"Wait." I put a hand on her arm. Keep her there while I call the concierge. Explain that Jennie will be heading up before me. To let her in. Only her.

I've never had a problem with security. My building is secure. No one gets in without clearance. But I have to make sure they let Jennie up to my condo.

I press my door key into her hand.

"Don't look at him," I say.

"How could I? I don't know what he looks like."

"Good. All the better. Now go."

I unlock the bathroom door, letting the line of women spill in.

They look at me, full of questions and irritation at holding up the bathroom. I don't care.

I stand against the wall. Waiting. Biding my time. Giving Jennie a head start.

I check the time on my phone. Five minutes. It's only been five minutes since I ducked in here, but it feels like an eternity.

It could easily take her five minutes to convince her new friend that she needs him to walk her home. She needs a good reason. I should have helped her with a reason. But she's smart. She'll think of something.

The women leave the restroom and more come in. I ignore them.

I'm just a girl hiding out in the restroom. It happens. For all they know, I'm hiding from an abusive boyfriend.

Doesn't matter.

I check the time again.

It's been ten minutes now.

I've been in here too long. Silas Crowe is going to wonder why I'm in here.

I quickly schedule an Uber. Two minutes out.

It'll take me two minutes to get out of here and meet the Uber outside.

If he followed me here, he already knows where I live.

Can't think about that right now. Anyway, I'm not walking outside by myself.

Leaving the restroom, I see him still sitting there in his out-of-place clothes. A girl with a ponytail is talking to him.

What's wrong with people? I may never go to a bar again.

It's too dangerous. Anyone could be lurking about. We joke about accidentally meeting serial killers at places like this. But it really does happen.

There really are killers among us and no one realizes it.

I feel obligated to warn her away from him.

But that obligation is overridden by my own survival instincts.

I step outside into the night air, still warm from the day's sunshine just as my Uber pulls up to the curb.

"The Galleria?" he asks.

"Yes." I sit back. Bide my time. Watch out the back window to see if anyone follows. They don't. Silas Crowe would not expect me to get into a car.

Patience is not easy in this situation.

I send Jennie a text.

> Are you home?

JENNIE
> Yes. Just got inside. Where are you?

> Lock the door.

"Something's come up," I tell my driver. Can you take me back downtown?"

FOUR

McKenna

Safely back in my condo, I crash onto the sofa and close my eyes.

"I'm so sorry about that," I tell Jennie who's texting her new friend. "What's his name?"

"James."

"What did you tell him?" I open my eyes and look at her.

"Just that something came up and my friend needed me."

"Vague enough."

"Don't worry about that." She sets her phone aside. "What are you going to do about that Silas guy?"

"I don't know yet. I'll talk to Miles tomorrow."

"Miles?"

"My boss. He'll know what to do. Not that there's anything we can do. But at least we'll have more information."

"I'm glad I'm staying here with you while I'm stateside."

"Me too. I'm going to get some sleep."

"Good idea." Jennie is texting again. She'll probably be up all night texting the guy. James. But I'm too exhausted to care. Besides, it's her business.

I'm the one with the serial killer tracking me down.

Jennie is just a girl doing her thing.

I go to the balcony door, lock it, and look out on the city that just hours ago had made me so happy. Now all I can think about is Silas Crowe being out there somewhere.

He's supposed to be behind bars.

"Do you really think he tracked you down?" Jennie asks. "Or do you think he just ended up here?"

"What are the odds of him just randomly showing up in bar below my condo?"

"Good point. I wonder how he got out of prison."

"I'll find out tomorrow. He won't be out long. He'll do something stupid and get himself thrown back in."

"I just hope he doesn't hurt anyone again."

"We have to be careful," I say.

"You might have to move. At least for awhile."

"I won't let him run me out of my home."

"Do what you have to do, McKenna. To stay alive." She sweeps a hand around my little condo. "It's just a place. I know it's yours and I know you're attached to it, but in the end, it's just a place."

"How did you get so wise?" I ask.

"I'm not wise," Jennie says. "You can remind me I said that when I finally have a place of my own."

"Don't worry. I'll remind you."

"Don't worry," Jennie says. "Whatever happens, everything will be okay."

"I know. You're the best."

I try not to think about how if Jennie hadn't wanted to go out, I wouldn't have seen Silas Crowe tonight.

It's not her fault. If he tracked me down, he would have found me somewhere else.

Maybe it's better that he found me in a public place instead finding me alone on a street.

Everything happens for a reason.

I just hate it that what had been such a good day had to end on a such a negative note.

But tomorrow will be another day.

Everything will look better tomorrow.

CHAPTER
FIVE

McKenna

Those first few moments after waking up in the morning are always the best part of any day.

In those few moments, everything seems right with the world.

Whatever troubles the day before held are held at bay by the remnants of sleep.

Unfortunately, what's left of sleep can only hold those memories back for so long before they all come crashing forward, making themselves the center of attention.

Today's calamity spilling over from yesterday is Silas Crowe.

The sweetness of sleep is pushed aside by the image of that man sitting across the bar. Watching me.

He had definitely been watching me. I'd tried to convince myself last night that I'd imagined it. In fact, that's how I'd managed to fall asleep to begin with.

But in the light of day, I know that I had not imagined it.

It was not random and I had not imagined it.

He had been downstairs and he had been watching me.

He had found me.

But I'd gotten us out of there. I had gotten both me and Jennie out of there.

We're in my secure condo. No one can get up here without authorization.

We're safe.

Like always, the first thing I do is check my phone.

Miles has sent me a new message.

MILES

Are you coming in the office today?
We can talk about Silas Crowe.

I'll be there.

I have no choice. I have to go in.

Miles will make some calls. Send some messages. Do whatever he does and find out how Silas Crowe got out of jail.

Then we can begin trying to figure out how to get him back behind bars where he belongs.

Silas Crowe is not fit for society. He needs to go back under the rock I put him under.

I shower and dress.

It's Saturday, so I put on khaki slacks and a new white button-down shirt. Put on my white sneakers.

I love going to the office on weekends. It's the best time to get work done. If not at the office, I work at home. Walking to the office, though, is a good excuse to stop for a designer coffee.

Jennie's door is ajar, so I peek inside. She's still sleeping.

Since I'm going out, I don't stop to make coffee for myself.

I grab a sticky note and write her a note. Tell her I'm going into the office. Keep the doors locked.

I know she knows, but I can't help myself.

Tell her to text me if she needs anything. Should be home for lunch.

I hate leaving her, but since she's going to be living here for a couple of months, we'll both have to get used to it.

I hold up a hand to wave at Edwardo as I pass the front desk. He has the phone pressed to his ear, but holds up a hand to wave back.

Stepping out onto the street is like stepping out into a different world.

The air is humid and smells like exhaust and Texas wind. A unique and familiar combination.

The morning sunlight glints off the tall glass buildings and the sky is a beautiful shade of pinks and light oranges.

I'm pleased to be part of the city vibe.

Two joggers, a man and a woman, pass by, both wearing shorts. Reminds me that I need to start jogging again. Exercise is so hard to start and so easy to stop.

It's Saturday morning, so not too many people are out and about. The metro train passes by. It has a few people on it. Going wherever they're going. To work. Home. A thousand different possibilities.

I don't have to ride the train to work. I turn right at the first corner and pass by the pizzeria, closed now, and head for the coffee shop.

Going by the coffee shop takes me the long way around to the office.

The coffee shop is crowded with people of all ages.

I recognize the barista, but the patrons, like always are different. I scan their faces, looking for Silas Crowe. I hate that I do that. But at this point it's automatic.

But it's best to be wary rather than stick my head in the sand like Silas isn't out here.

I order my usual. A venti vanilla latte with extra vanilla and caramel drizzle. Whole milk.

Then I step aside to wait. Like everyone else in the coffee shop, I open up my phone and scan my messages. Email is quiet on a Saturday morning. It won't stay that way. Most attorneys don't take weekends off.

Ha. Like I do.

I work seven days a week.

The slowing of messages is typically barely noticeable.

The only thing that really slows down is the number of messages from the offices, which are closed.

"McKenna," the barista slides my coffee toward me.

"Thanks, Henry" I say. "Have a good day."

"Don't work too hard."

After sampling my coffee, I head back out onto the street and make my way around to the office. I pass beneath a covered construction area. Orange tape flutters in the breeze and the buzz of vibrating concrete drills has me hurrying past.

After scanning my card to get inside the office building, I step into an entirely different world. This one sleek and modern.

The lobby is about a mile wide. Sleek chandeliers. Little sofas gathered into private waiting areas. A concierge discretely watching everything.

Another scan to get up the elevator.

Security is everything.

The quiet elevator takes me up to the forty-first floor. Another lobby. This one also quiet and dignified, everything understated.

The halls are quiet as always, but they feel quieter on a Saturday morning without the receptionists there to monitor everything and greet us.

I walk straight into Miles' office and sit down in one of the two leather chairs in front of his desk.

"Good morning," he says. Miles is dressed like he always dresses. Designer suit. Perfect haircut. This morning, though, his tie is loosened, like he's been tugging on it.

"Have you found out what happened?" I ask in lieu of greeting.

"Not yet." He's wearing a perpetual scowl. He's barely forty years old, but already he has permanently creased brow lines that shouldn't be there yet.

His job is hard. I wouldn't want it.

"Theories?" I ask.

"I have some calls out. We should know something by the end of the day."

"I saw him," I say.

"When?" A flicker of surprise crosses his features.

"Last night."

"Where?"

"At a bar across the street from my building. I don't normally go to bars," I clarify quickly. "But my friend Jennie just got back in country and she wanted the company. I was sitting there having a glass of sparkling water, waiting for her."

"You don't have to justify yourself to me."

"I just want you to know details. I wasn't drinking. I was watching Jennie on the dance floor. That's when I saw him sitting behind her. He didn't fit in. The only blue collar guy in a bar full of professionals. Wearing what looked like a uniform, but I couldn't make out the details."

"He saw you?"

"I'm certain he did."

Miles leans back in his chair, laces his fingers behind his neck. "It can't be random."

"I know. It's too much to be random."

"You're not going to like what I have to say."

"Tell me anyway." I brace myself. Miles is the smartest attorney I know. If anybody can figure this thing out, he can.

"We need to put you in Witness Protection."

"What?" My stomach drops. "Witness Protection." I shake my head. "No."

"I warned you."

"You're just tossing that out there like it's nothing." Like *take a new case. It's no big deal.*

"Silas Crowe is not nothing."

"But..." Witness Protection would kill my career. It would kill my chances at ever being a judge.

"The main thing is to keep you alive."

I've heard him say these words to other people before. But not to me.

Not to me.

"Miles. No." Tears spring to my eyes. I blink them back and keep my chin held high. "My career."

He holds up his right hand. "Your career." Then holds up his left hand. "Your life."

"There must be another solution. Something that doesn't involve completely destroying my life."

"Maybe," he says, dragging his glasses off his perfectly

chiseled face. But I know he's placating me. He doesn't mean it.

He's already decided that Witness Protection is my best solution.

My phone chimes with Jennie's ring tone.

I look at the message.

JENNIE

> There's a leak in the kitchen. The ceiling. Water is coming down like rain. What do I do?

> I'll call the concierge.

"There's a leak in my condo. I just need to..."

"Go ahead," Miles says, waving away my apology. "Take care of it."

I call the concierge. "There's a leak in my kitchen."

"Yes ma'am. We'll go right up and check it out." A pause. "Actually it'll be a few minutes."

I text Jennie back.

> They're sending someone up to check on it. You'll have to let them in.

JENNIE

Okay. No problem. Thanks.

> Thank you. I'll come back. Deal with it.

JENNIE

No. I can handle it. Do your work
thing.

"Okay," I say, looking back up at Miles. "You really think it's that serious? Serious enough for me to have to give up everything?"

"You know he killed his girlfriend. He threatened you."

"Maybe I shouldn't have told you that."

"We'll compromise," Miles says. "We'll wait until I hear back from my sources. Find out what he's doing out. Find out how they plan to put him back in prison. Then we'll discuss it further."

"Okay."

"But in the meantime, you need to be seriously considering your options."

"You mean my lack of options."

"Keep your safety in mind."

"I'll be in my office if you hear anything."

"You'll be the first to know."

CHAPTER
SIX

McKenna

I sit at my desk. Take care of some routine paperwork.

But in truth, my thoughts are not focused on my work.

Instead, I look around my little office. Not a corner, but it has floor-to-ceiling windows. Not bad for a junior partner.

My glass top desk has nothing on it but a computer and a little lamp.

Behind me, the credenza has stacks of paperwork.

Standing up, I walk to the window and look outside. Rain clouds bruise the sky to the south. I can't remember the last time I checked a weather report.

There could be a hurricane in the gulf and unless

someone told me, I wouldn't even know it. Correction. We'd get an email telling us about it. I'm not the only attorney who keeps my head down and focused.

Today, though, I'm not focused.

Miles wants me to give up everything and go into the Witness Protection program.

My parents wouldn't notice. They're doing their own thing. Living their life. My brothers probably would only notice in passing. One lives in Boston. One lives in Portugal.

Family ties are not our strong suit. In this particular situation, that's an advantage.

I would have to give up Jennie. That's the worst of it, as far as people go.

Then there's my condo. I'd get over it.

But my job.

I would not get over giving up my job and my dream of being a judge.

Refusing to let myself accept that Witness Protection is the only option, I go back to my desk and sit down.

I haven't heard from Jennie lately.

I send her a quick text.

> Did anyone come by yet to take care of the leak?

She doesn't answer.

Probably went back to bed. Or maybe she's talking to her new friend. Maybe she met him for breakfast.

Silas Crowe doesn't know about her, so she should be okay.

I'm the one he's after.

I'm the one who is going to have my entire life turned upside down because of him.

There has to be another solution.

He's supposed to be in prison. He'll go back to prison.

I just have to stay safe until that happens.

I finish off my coffee and drop the cup in the wastebasket. Open up my computer and start reviewing some files on a case I'm working on.

Check my phone.

Still not word from Jennie.

The least she could do is send me a text. It would only take a second.

Feeling annoyed, I close my computer and slide it aside.

I run my hands through my hair.

There's no way I'm going to get any work done this morning.

I look up to find Miles standing in my doorway.

"You heard something," I say.

He sits down in one of my two chairs. "Yes."

"What did you hear?"

"They let him out on a technicality."

"Wait. A what? A technicality?"

"Yes."

"No. We had this thing sewed up. There were no technicalities. What was it?"

"Still waiting to hear back about that."

I push back in my chair. Stand up and walk to the window.

No answers there.

I whirl back around to look at Miles.

"He's not going back to prison is he?"

"You already know the answer to that question."

I want him to lie to me. To tell me that Silas Crowe is indeed going back to prison. That he'll find a way to make it happen.

"Is that it?" I ask. "Is that all you have right now?"

"I'm afraid so. The Witness Protection Rep will come by Monday morning to meet with us. I suggest you go home. Get some rest. Do some thinking."

"Right." I drop back down in my chair. "Do some thinking."

"You have to take this seriously," Miles says.

"I take everything seriously."

"I know you do."

"I need to go check on Jennie anyway. She hasn't responded to my texts."

Miles quickly hides an expression of alarm, but I see it anyway.

"She's that way. Easily distracted."

"Go. Go check on your friend."

"I'm taking work home with me," I say. "I have some billing to do."

"Fine. I'll text you. Let you know what time the meeting with the Witness Protection rep is Monday."

"Right. The meeting." I unplug the computer. Toss the charging cords into my computer bag along with my computer.

I scan the stacks of papers of my credenza. Decide they can wait. Most of what I need to do is on my computer anyway.

"Don't try to do too much," Miles says. "You need to be thinking about what we talked about."

"Witness Protection."

He holds up a hand. "Your career." He holds up the other hand. "Your life."

"Stop that," I say. "Look for something in the middle. You always tell me to look for the hidden option. So. Look for the hidden option."

"I'll look," he says, but I know he won't. He's already decided.

"Would you do it?" I ask, tossing a new legal pad into my computer bag. "Would you join Witness Protection because of this? Because of Silas Crowe?"

"I might."

"You might. Then assume that you're talking about your life and your career. Figure out some other way."

"I told you I would think about it," he says. "But I need you to think about it, too."

"I'll think about it," I say, unable to hide the distress in my voice. It's the only thing I'll be thinking about. I already know that.

One day I'm going along enjoying my life. The next day, I'm being told I have go into permanent hiding.

It happens that way. That's how it happens.

It's not like planning a vacation. It's sudden and it's disruptive.

But right now I need to get home and check on my friend.

Then I can figure out how to keep Silas Crowe from destroying my entire way of life.

CHAPTER
SEVEN

McKenna

Jennie doesn't pick up her phone. Doesn't answer her text.

To say that I'm annoyed with her is an understatement. If she went somewhere and didn't tell me.... Or if she has that guy over...

I walk underneath the construction zone. The buzz of the vibrating concrete drills and the fluttering orange tape. The metro rail rings its bell as it zips past.

A homeless person, humming softly to himself, sits on a concrete slab, hoping someone will drop a dollar in his upturned hat.

Normal, everyday city noises.

I slide my phone in my pocket and turn left toward my building.

Jennie is a grown woman.

But she said she'd take care of the water leak. It's not the first time there's been a water leak in my condo. Comes with the territory of living in a high rise. Everyone's units are connected.

I push open the door and step inside the lobby.

The scent of fresh daisies replaces the scent of outdoors.

Juan is standing behind the desk, several newly delivered packages in front of him, including someone's pizza delivery.

"Hey Juan. Did they take care of the leak?"

Juan looks perplexed. "I just came on my shift," he says.

"I talked to Edwardo. He was supposed to send someone up to take a look."

"Let me check." He taps on the computer keys. Frowns. "Says no one answered the door."

I shake my head. "Does it show that I called about the leak?"

"Sure," he says. "I'll come up. Check it out myself."

"No. That's okay." I pull my hair back. Let it fall down my back. "You've got deliveries to make. I'm heading up. I'll check it out. I'll call you. Let you know."

"Okay, Miss McKenna. Just let me know what I need to do."

I step onto the elevator and wait while it carries me up

to my floor. They posted a new flyer. There's a book club meeting coming up.

I wouldn't have time to attend the meeting, not to even mention reading the book.

It's amazing to me that people have time for these kinds of leisure activities.

The elevator doors open and I step off into my hallway. Walk down to my condo.

So quiet. It's always so quiet. Sometimes I forget other people actually live in the building.

I open the door to my condo and step inside.

"Jennie?" I call out. My voices echoes through the empty condo.

I put my hands on my hips. She left without telling me. She obviously did not take me seriously about staying inside, at least until we figure out something about Silas Crowe.

If I have to leave here, which it's looking like I will, one way or another, then she'll have to leave, too.

Even if I'm just moving across town, it's best if she gets a place of her own. Best if she disassociates from me for the time being.

I slide my phone out of my pocket and dial Jennie's number.

Overprotective.

I'm such an overprotective friend.

Even though I'm mad at her, I—

Her phone rings. I hear the ring tone she gave me. Ringing.

"Jennie?"

I take a step forward. It sounds like maybe it's coming from the kitchen.

As I near the counter leading into the kitchen, I see water on the floor.

I glance up toward the ceiling, but it's dry now. The leak must have stopped on its own.

My white sneakers splash in a puddle of water, drawing my gaze back down.

Walking carefully now, I step around the counter, giving me a full view of the kitchen.

Jennie lying face down on the floor. Her arms outstretched. Her phone in a puddle of dirty water.

But the water isn't dirty.

It isn't... water exactly.

It's... blood?

Blood.

"Jennie!" I drop to my knees next to her. "Jennie."

I grab her arm, but she doesn't move.

"No. No. No."

Using all my strength, I roll her over. "Jennie. Wake up. Jennie."

But her eyes.

I know from looking at crime scene photos that Jennie isn't going to wake up.

But this isn't a crime scene. This is Jennie.

"Jennie. No. Jennie." I can't catch my breath.

There's blood everywhere. It's all over my white shirt.

I have to do something.

What am I supposed to do?

Call 911. I'm supposed to call 911.

There's blood everywhere.

Shutting off my emotions, forcing myself to be logical, I look for the source of the blood.

Stabbed. Jennie was stabbed in the stomach.

Silas Crowe.

But how?

How did Silas Crowe get up here?

My knees trembling, I stand up. Walk through my condo. Looking for what, I don't know.

Contaminating the crime scene.

I have to get out of here.

I leave my condo and walk down the hallway toward the elevators.

I don't know where I'm going. I'm not going anywhere.

Just away. Away from here.

As I reach the bank of elevators, the one in the middle opens and Juan steps off.

"My God. McKenna," he says. "What happened?"

"It's Jennie," I say. "Jennie. She…"

The floor is moving beneath me. I reach out a hand to steady myself, but Juan is there, keeping me from falling onto the floor.

He helps me to the bench in front of the elevators.

"Lean your head forward," he says.

I do as he says. Then I hear him on the phone. Calling 911.

I should have called 911.

Jennie.

I left her alone and he got to her.

This is my fault.

"Is there someone I can call?" Juan asks, sitting next to me now.

"No. Miles. You can call Miles."

I put my phone in his hand.

Miles will know what to do.

CHAPTER
EIGHT

The rest of the day passes in a blur.

Policemen scour my condo. They take a lot of photos. Ask a lot of questions.

Miles keeps me distracted while someone comes and takes Jennie away.

I need to call her parents.

Miles will do it.

Miles will take care of calling Jennie's parents.

Without Miles, I wouldn't be functional.

Not that I'm functional now.

Miles presses a bottle of water into my hands. "Drink," he says.

I do as he says.

Then he's pacing. Talking to someone again. On the phone.

I zone in and out.

People come and go. In and out of my condo. I mostly ignore them.

"You can't stay here," Miles says, talking to me now. "Your home is a crime scene."

"Okay." I know that. Of course I do.

"McKenna," he says. "Listen to me. You're going to take a shower. Put on clean clothes. Then we're going to pack a bag for you. You have to leave here."

"I'll get a hotel," I say.

"No. You'll come with me. To my home. My wife and I have a guest room. You'll stay with us."

"No. I can't. I can't put you in danger." It feels like the most logical thought I've had in hours.

"We'll be okay," he says. "I can't leave you alone."

"Okay," I say, looking at my hands, still covered in blood.

"Will you be okay to go shower? Go get cleaned up?"

"No choice," I say. "I have no choice."

"Good. Go. I'll be right here when you get out."

I walk past the guest room—Jennie's room, to my own bedroom and close the door.

It's all surreal.

Focus. I have to focus.

All I have to do is take a shower. Put on clean clothes.

It's not that big a task.

I turn on the hot water in the shower and, hands trembling, wash my hands in the sink while the water heats. Blood, Jennie's blood, washes off my skin.

With clean hands now, I pull out clean clothes. Jeans and a t-shirt.

The clothes I'm wearing are ruined. Evidence. They're evidence now.

As I step into the shower, my prosecutor brain goes to work.

Jennie was stabbed. But there was no weapon. It had not been an accident.

Murder.

Jennie was murdered.

In my kitchen.

It was Silas Crowe. I'm certain of it.

But how could he possibly get inside my condo?

Something about the way he was dressed last night flits through my brain, but the thought is gone before it registers.

Out of the shower. Dressed. My brain is back on autopilot.

Get dressed. Pack.

I don't know when I'll be back here again.

Miles knocks on my door. "McKenna? Are you okay?"

I open the door. "Just packing."

"Can I help?" he asks, looking toward my closet. "You left your shoes."

I follow his gaze and it occurs to me that I have managed to pack all my clothes into two suitcases. But I left my shoes.

"I'll get a box for your shoes," he says, on the phone again.

As I finish transferring the contents of my dresser to my suitcase, Edwardo comes to my bedroom door with a trolley and a stack of folded boxes.

It's Edwardo's shift again? So much time has slipped by. A glance at the window tells me it's dark outside. How did that happen?

Miles builds one of the boxes and carefully packs my shoes, putting towels in between them.

"Toiletries," he says, handing me a pink bag he finds in my closet.

I take the bag into the bathroom and fill it with everything from shampoo and conditioner to makeup and lotions.

When I'm finished, it looks like I've moved out. I toss my damp towel into the hamper and roll it out, too.

Miles and Juan stop talking and just look at me.

I straighten my shoulders. "I don't know when I'll be back," I say.

"It's okay," Miles says. "You're right. Bring everything." He turns to Edwardo. "Would you check the rest of the unit. See if there's anything else personal she needs to bring? Put it in this box." He puts a folded box in Edwardo's hands.

"We should go," Miles tells me. "Are you ready?"

"My clothes. Are in the bathroom. For evidence."

"Good. We'll get them later." He hangs my bag of toiletries on the trolley along with my two suitcases and two boxes full of shoes.

As he leads me down the hallway toward my living room, I know what he's thinking. He's thinking that he's going to put me in Witness Protection.

I'm not going. I don't trust the system.

But I'm not ready to tell him that.

Right now I just want to get out of this condo.

My gaze strays toward the kitchen as we walk past. Someone cleaned up the mess. I don't know when, but someone cleaned it up.

A lump forms in my throat.

Jenny. Jenny should be here with me.

I was supposed to keep her safe, but I didn't.

Because of me, Jennie is gone.

"Do you need anything out of there?" Miles asks.

Holding my head high, I swallow the lump in my throat.

"No." Whatever it is, I want nothing to do with it.

As we walk out the door, there's one thing I'm certain of.

I won't be coming back here again.

McKenna

When I wake, it's still nighttime.

I roll over and reach for my phone on my nightstand, but it's not my nightstand.

I'm in Miles's guest room.

And date on my phone tells me that it's not just night-time, it's a day later. I slept through an entire day.

I'd fallen into bed, numb and exhausted, on Saturday night. It's eight o'clock on Sunday night.

I've never done that. Maybe once when I'd had the flu as a kid, but never as an adult.

I lost a whole day.

And Jennie is gone.

It would be so easy to just roll over and go back to sleep. Sleep through another day.

As long as I'm asleep, I don't have to deal with anything.

I don't have to think about Jennie.

I don't have to think about Silas Crowe.

I don't have to think about how my life has been turned upside down.

Throwing my legs over the side of the bed, I sit up. Dizzy. I'm a little lightheaded. Probably from not eating in two days.

Mile's wife, Tabby, made me a grilled cheese last night. I think I ate maybe about a fourth of it.

I'm surprised they let me sleep all day. Maybe they knew I needed to sleep more than anything else.

I don't even remember changing into my pajamas last night. I'd definitely been operating on autopilot.

I pull on the jeans and t-shirt I'd worn over here last night and venture out of my room.

Miles and Tabby have one of those nice houses on Memorial. I've been to their house before, but I've never been upstairs until last night.

The hallway is in shadows but moonlight spills in through the acres of unadorned glass at either end of the hallway and I easily find my way to the top of the stairs.

I follow the sound of the television to the living room. Stop in the doorway and hesitate. The two of them are curled up together under a blanket on the sofa. Not sure if I should disturb them or go in search of something to eat on my own.

Tabby sees me, says something to Miles, and he pauses the television.

"I don't mean to disturb," I say. "But—"

"Nonsense," Tabby says, getting up. "You must be starving."

"I'm a little hungry," I say, with a little forced smile.

"I saved you some pasta," Tabby says as I follow her into the kitchen. She flips on the light.

"You're so kind," I say, feeling my eyes welling up as I remember why I'm here and why she's being so kind.

"Think nothing of it," Tabby says. "Have a seat. I'll heat it up."

I sit at one of the bar stools.

Miles comes to the door. "Feeling rested?" he asks me.

"A little," I say. "I should any way. I don't think I've ever slept for twenty-four hours."

"Understandable," he says. "Feel like riding into the office with me tomorrow?"

Tabby looks at him with a little shake of her head. He shrugs.

"Sure." But I cast my gaze down. I already know what he's up to.

"The Witness Protection rep will be there at ten to talk to you."

And I was right about that. The microwave beeps and

Tabby pulls my plate out. Sets it front of me along with a fork.

"I can just meet you there," I say. "I don't know if I'll be up early enough to ride in with you."

Tabby and Miles exchange a look. It's obvious they've been talking about me.

Obvious and normal. Of course they have. I was asleep in their guest room for twenty-four hours. Not normal.

I take a bite of the delicious pasta. Miles always brags about his wife being a good cook. Can't argue with that.

"I don't mind waiting," Miles says.

"Miles," Tabby says. "Just let her drive in."

Miles holds up his hands. "Okay. If you feel up to it."

"If I'm not up when you leave, just go without me."

"Okay," Miles says. "I'm going down the hall to my office for a few minutes."

Tabby sits down next to me. "When he says he's going to the office for a few minutes, he usually means a few hours."

"It's not intentional. It just comes with the territory. This is so good."

"Miles likes you. He's always said you're one of the best young attorneys he's known."

I take a deep breath. She's trying to be nice.

"He wants me to go into Witness Protection." She obviously already knows that.

"I know."

"If I do, I can't practice law anymore."

"I know."

I put my fork down and look at her. "Then why? Why would he want me to give that up?"

"He likes you."

A circular argument. "He acts like it's no big deal."

"He knows it's a big deal. He also knows it's the only thing that will keep you safe from Silas Crowe."

"He knows something I don't."

She looks away, confirming my suspicion. Straightens yellow daisies in a vase on the counter in front of us.

"I'll talk to them," I say. "But I already know what she's going to say. I've heard the spiel."

"I know you have," Tabby says. "It's just important for you to stay alive. Whatever you do."

Stay alive. Whatever you do.

So much like one of the last things Jennie said to me. "Do what you have to do, McKenna. To stay alive."

Maybe I'm missing something.

I think about the three people I've referred to Witness Protection during my career. They probably felt blindsided just like I do. They even asked me for other options. I never had one.

Having the shoe on the other foot, so to speak, is not a pleasant feeling.

"I'll meet with them," I say. "You can let Miles know I'll hear what they have to say."

"Good," Tabby says, obviously relieved.

Doesn't mean I'm going to do it. It just means I'll meet with them.

"But I'm tired now," I say. "Do you mind if I go back to my room?"

"Of course not, Dear. If you need anything at all, just come and find me."

"I will. Thank you again for being so kind."

She takes my plate before I can put it away myself.

As I leave her kitchen, I have an uncharacteristically strong urge to call my parents. My family might not be close, but we're still family.

Right now, Tabby and Miles are the closest thing I have to family and that makes me miss my family all the more. But I know it's not smart to call them. The less they know the better.

CHAPTER
TEN

McKenna

I leave the office the next day at eleven thirty.

The Witness Protection Agent, a young lady named Eleanor, was kind and knowledgeable. The initial meetings usually take several hours, but mine was short because I didn't have questions. I already know the drill.

I know how it works.

She went over everything anyway. Miles sat in on the meeting. He'd already let her know that this wasn't anything new to me.

But Eleanor was young and she had her presentation to run through.

It's like that when you're young. You don't know how to

jump around. You don't know which parts to leave out without losing your place.

It was obvious that she wanted me to leave with her now. To go to the Witness Protection's private, secret office and start the ball rolling.

But I told her I'd let her know by the end of the day and if I decided to enter the program, I'd meet her at her office tomorrow.

It's not that I have so much to think about. I know the pros and cons and all that. I know they can keep me safe if I change my name, let them send me someplace far away with a new identity including a new career. I know all that.

It's just that I don't want to go. I don't want to give up my career. I have plans for my life. Big plans. And everything has been going along nicely.

I know that I'm not the first attorney to deal with this kind of thing. But despite Tabby's admission that Miles knows something he's not telling me, whatever it is, he's keeping it to himself.

I borrowed Miles' key and knowing that Tabby is working today, I head straight to their house.

I run a load of laundry and make myself a sandwich.

It's a good thing I don't have a lot to think about because my thoughts are all over the place.

While my laundry dries, I repack my suitcases, layering in several pairs of shoes and filling a box with clothes to donate.

Getting organized usually helps me organize my

thoughts. Unfortunately, instead of clarifying what I need to do, it just leaves me feeling more confused and unsettled.

As I pull my clothes out of the dryer, my phone chimes with a text message.

An unknown number.

I almost delete it as just another spam message, but something catches my attention and I open it up to read it.

UNKNOWN

Don't think you can hide. Wherever you go, I will find you. If nothing else, your new friends will tell me where to find you.

I stare at the message, my heart rate galloping about a thousand beats a minute.

My new friends.

He means Tabby and Miles.

It's from Silas Crowe. I have no doubt about that.

I type out a response.

Leave them alone.

But I delete it and don't send anything.

I don't respond.

My hands shaking, I fold and pack my still warm clothes fresh out of the dryer. Fold my towel and put it in my giveaway box. My two suitcases are full.

There are some things, like my towels, that I have to let go of.

They don't fit in my suitcase and as such, they aren't going to fit in my new life.

I zip up one suitcase, then the next. Stand them up and roll them to the garage door where my car is parked.

My scattered thoughts are starting to come together, like pieces of a puzzle.

Turns out there is another solution.

One that should keep everyone safe.

I take out a sheet of paper and write a note for Tabby and Miles.

They, at least, deserve an explanation. And they can tell my family.

They might want *me* to do whatever it takes to keep *me* safe, but my task is also to keep others safe.

I failed in that with Jennie. I won't fail anyone else.

Jennie didn't deserve to die just because of her association with me.

And no one else does either.

I'll do whatever it takes to keep anyone else associated with me safe.

That includes not only my family, but also Miles and Tabby.

CHAPTER
ELEVEN

MᴄKᴇɴɴᴀ

Rᴀɪɴ ɪs ᴄᴏᴍɪɴɢ down in sheets and my windshield wipers are no match for the steady downpour.

An eighteen wheeler passes me on the left, tossing even more water onto my already overstressed windshield wipers.

My hands ache from squeezing the steering wheel like my life depends upon it and I think it might very well do so.

I keep thinking I'll be out of the rain soon, but it's not letting up.

Seeing the lights of a diner through the downfall, I pull over and park my car around the side of the building behind a big pickup truck. No one would be able to see my car from the four lane highway. Not even if it wasn't raining.

Not that anyone knows where I am.

I open up my phone and check the weather first. Whatever storm I'm in must be following me. It's not letting up. Maybe that's what I get for traveling east. Storms, at least this particular one, travel east, too.

After checking the weather, I check my GPS. I'm somewhere in west Tennessee.

After driving around Houston for three hours, I'd left the city limits and headed west for awhile. Then north. Then east.

Unless Silas Crowe has a tracker on my car, he has no way of knowing where I am.

I don't think he could possibly have put a tracker on my car, but I also didn't think there was any way he could have gotten into my condo building without detection.

Tomorrow, after the rain lets up, I'll visit a used car lot and trade in my car.

Getting into a different car will take away any possibility that Silas could be tracking me.

No one knows where I am. I haven't answered a single phone call in the nearly two days I've been on the road.

Miles called half a dozen times. I had some calls that I didn't answer. Those were easy. Not answering Miles's calls was anything but easy. He and his wife had been so kind to me. And on top of that, I'd left him with taking care of everything concerning Jennie.

But this way he doesn't know where I am and he can't try to convince me to go back to Houston.

I haven't gotten any more threatening messages from Silas, aka the unknown caller.

It makes me wonder if he was watching me.

The thought sends a chill down my spine. I turn around and look behind me, but there's nothing to see other than torrents of rain coming down.

I need to wait out the storm, driving right now is both unsafe and exhausting. And I really have to go to the bathroom. On top of that, I'm hungry. So this is the perfect place for me to stop for awhile.

I open my door and pop my umbrella up. My purse zipped up and over my shoulder, I step out of the car.

Splashing through puddles, I make my way around to the front door of the diner.

Apparently three o'clock is the perfect time to eat here. Other than two older couples on either side of the restaurant, I'm the only customer.

"Oh my goodness," a young lady with big bleached hair and bright red lipstick says. "Come in out of that rain. Sit anywhere you want to. You want some coffee?"

"Coffee would be nice. Thank you. Restroom?"

"Right through that door Hon," she says. Traci. According to her name tag.

After a quick trip to the restroom, I sit at a booth not far from the door. The seats are worn leather, but comfortable and clean.

"You look like you've been traveling for awhile," Traci says.

"That bad, huh?" I shove my hair back.

"Not that," she says. "It's the eyes." She points to her own. "They get what I call road glazed."

"Road glazed. That's about how I feel."

"We have fresh apple pie if you'd like some."

I almost reflexively say no to the pie. But why not? "Sure. Sounds good."

With a smile, Traci leaves me to check on her other customers and get my slice of pie.

I pull out my phone and study the map. It makes sense to me to trade in my car, then change direction again.

I look up used car lots near me. There are two.

Although I've never bought a used car—I've always bought new cars—my experience with dealerships is it always takes longer than it should. I can't imagine that being any different buying a used car than a new one.

A glance out the window tells me this is not a good time to go looking at cars. A flash of lightning slams against the window followed almost immediately by a rumble of thunder.

Or maybe it is.

Traci drops off my pie. "Fresh out of the oven," she says.

"Thank you Traci."

The pie tastes homemade. Big chunks of crisp apples and flaky crust.

My stomach drops as an unknown text message comes in on my phone.

Lowering my fork, I tap my phone to read it.

UNKNOWN

You can run, but you can't hide, my little mouse.

I think I'm going to be sick. I shove my plate back. I definitely can't eat any more pie right now.

UNKNOWN

Your little friend didn't even see me coming. I hope you'll be more of a challenge.

I shove my phone away and lean back against the seat.

"You okay, Hon?" Traci asks, standing at my table again, looking genuinely concerned.

I look up at her, my eyes wide.

"I swear. You look like you've seen a ghost."

"No," I say. "It's just... It's nothing. But I have to go. Can I pay you now?" I slide my phone back toward me and turn it over. "I have to go."

"Oh dear. And with this weather. Just go. Don't worry about paying."

"But I—"

"No ma'am. It's on the house. Just be careful out there."

It's baffling how there can be so much good in the

world and so much evil at the same time. Something I honestly don't expect to ever understand.

CHAPTER

TWELVE

McKenna

Two days later, on a sunny afternoon, I'm driving my new-to-me 2018 Toyota SUV.

The little town where I'd bought my new vehicle didn't have a lot to choose from and the salesman had been perplexed enough to move things along quicker than usual. First of all, nobody in their right mind goes car shopping in the rain. And second, I didn't have to pay anything. They gave me a check for the difference between my two year old car and the SUV I drove off the lot.

This older SUV most definitely drives differently. The steering is looser, but I do like the way I'm sitting up above most all the others cars. It would have been good to be driving it during the rain storm.

But as luck would have it, the storm had moved out and I had headed north, then west, ending up on Interstate 70. An exceptionally boring drive, especially with no one to talk to.

I refused to call anyone I know. I refuse to give anyone any idea about where I am. Selfish? Maybe. But in the end, I'm doing it for unselfish reasons.

I could have just gone into Witness Protection. Maybe it would have been easier. Easier, but permanent. Once a person enters that system, it's for life.

It's not only permanent, but potentially trackable.

This way no one knows where I am. There's something decidedly freeing about that.

As I drive along the Interstate, it seems like I'm watching the Rocky Mountains for days.

Fascinating how they're visible from so far away.

Having never been to Colorado or anywhere in the mountains, I'm drawn to them.

Somehow the mountains are starting to feel like a good place to hide. So different from Houston. I can't imagine anyone looking for me out here.

I actually don't have cell phone service for most of the day.

On a whim, I turn north again and spend the night in a little hotel near the Wyoming border. I grab some fast food tacos and eat them in my hotel room as I study the map on my phone. Maybe I'll head over to Oregon. I follow the route on my phone, zooming in on the Oregon coast. I had an online professor once who lived on the Oregon coast. Might be interesting to check it out. See what it's all about.

Maybe I'll just stay on the road for the foreseeable future. But, honestly, I'm getting tired.

I'd like to land someplace and stay there for awhile. I was never a fan of traveling and any curiosity about traveling I might ever have had is completely out of my system.

I check the Houston news. Read about Jennie's murder. Fortunately, there's nothing about anyone else. Maybe Silas Crowe decided to leave me alone.

After I finish eating, I take a walk around the hotel grounds. Find a treadmill and walk for thirty minutes.

This is so not the life I saw for myself.

I entertain myself with thoughts about Silas Crowe going back to prison and me going back to my old life in Houston.

Picking up where I left off and becoming a judge.

It's still possible.

After my walk, I go back to my room and change into my pajamas.

I hardly ever even check my phone anymore. I consider it an addiction well-broken.

As I climb into bed, though, I plug it in to charge it and there's a text message front and center.

Hands shaking, I unlock my phone and read the message.

UNKNOWN

Do you really think you'll be safe on the Oregon coast? There's no place you can go that I can't find you.

I stare at the message, shock running through me.

How?

How could Silas possibly know I was thinking about Oregon? Was he in my head now?

My phone.

He's somehow tracking my phone.

I pick up my phone and toss it across the room. It hits the wall and lands quietly on the carpet.

He hadn't been tracking my car. He'd been tracking my phone.

He had somehow gotten into my phone.

So everything I looked at on my phone, he saw it too?

If that's the case, then he knows exactly where I am. He knows everything. He even knows what kind of car I'm driving now.

I'm not safe.

I should have gone into Witness Protection.

Miles had been right.

I'm not safe.

CHAPTER
THIRTEEN

McKenna

THE NEXT MORNING I drive off another used car lot. This time I'm driving a 2015 BMW sedan. Low mileage. The car salesman convinced me that BMWs are timeless. They run forever, he'd told me.

I'm not really sure I care right now what I drive.

I'm still reeling from the very real possibility that Silas Crowe knows what I was looking at on my phone. He somehow mirrored my phone.

Well. That won't be happening again.

Before I traded in my SUV, I stopped at a little park in Casper, Wyoming and tossed my phone into the river.

Take that, Silas Crowe. You won't be tracking me anymore.

He doesn't even know I have a different car.

And since Oregon is now no longer an option, I head south again, back toward Denver.

I'm so sick of driving. So sick of traveling.

I don't ever want to take another road trip.

After grabbing some lunch in Denver, I circle around heading west toward the mountains.

I feel like the mountains have been my destination all along.

It's an odd feeling, considering that I've not only never been to Colorado before, but I didn't set out to go here.

I get back on Interstate 70 and for a little while, I'm on the same route as the Amtrak. Sleek silver train cars winding their way through the mountains.

That's when it occurs to me that I don't need a car at all.

If Silas Crowe found a way to hack into my phone, he probably has a way to track my car purchases.

Making myself a little dizzy, I exit, turn around and head back to Denver. I won't lie. Finding my way around without my phone is a bit of a challenge. Fortunately, the car has a GPS system that is somewhat helpful.

I leave the new-to-me car in a Denver airport parking lot, then get an Uber to the Amtrak train station and, bringing both my suitcases with me, I use cash to buy myself a ticket to California.

Not that I plan to go to California, but if anyone, Silas

Crowe in particular, somehow happens to find out I bought a ticket, he'll have every reason to think I'm heading to California.

I don't know how he or anyone could possibly think I'm on a train. The car at the airport should be a dead end for anyone and everyone looking for me, if they get that far.

Finally, sitting in my seat on the train, I take in a breath and slowly let it out.

My car will remain parked at the airport. From the airport, I could go anywhere in the world. I have no cell phone.

I am completely and utterly untrackable.

Safe. I am safe.

I close my eyes and as the train starts moving, I fall asleep.

I wake up as the train slows at a little train station high in the mountains.

Someone behind me has a window open. The air feels different. Lighter. And it smells unbelievable clean and spicy. Like a candle shop at Christmastime.

Standing up, I stretch and look out at the little town high in the mountains surrounded by even higher mountains as far as the eye can see.

"Can we get off here?" I ask the conductor as he passes by.

"You can get off wherever you want to," he says.

"Can I get my luggage?"

He looks a bit exasperated at that, but says. "Sure. Do you have your ticket?"

I reach into my pocket and pull out my luggage ticket. Place it in his hand. "Thank you so much."

"Just doing my job," he says.

And not so very happy about it, obviously.

"Thank you," I say, heading down the aisle to get off the train.

Stepping off the train, I stand there a moment and look around.

Everything appears to be in slow motion.

No one is rushing to get anywhere.

There are trees everywhere.

Spruce trees and fir trees. Maple trees. Aspen trees.

And colorful flowers hanging out of hanging baskets.

In that moment I feel a twinge that I forgot my grandmother's ivy. Left it on the balcony of my condo.

Maybe Miles rescued it. I hope. If not, there's nothing I can do about it now. Perhaps it will at least rain to keep it alive until I can get back to it.

The little plant is the first thing that has truly tempted me to call Miles about.

I'm not sure what that says about me, but I need to think about it before I do that.

I could call the office and leave a message for him.

Tempting. I'll think on it.

Right now I need to orient myself to this little town.

I'm going to be staying here for awhile.

FOURTEEN

Caleb Lawson

"I need you to run some things out to the campground," Rachel says as I finish hauling a stack of cardboard boxes out of the back storage room of the Lawson Outfitter's Supply Store.

"Camping gear or survival kits?" I ask.

"Neither," she says, grabbing a box cutter and getting to work opening boxes. "Fishing supplies."

Lawson Outfitter's Supply Store is the largest store downtown Alpine Falls. Situated right in the middle of Main Street. We carry everything from tents to first aid kits to hand-knit hats and t-shirts.

My sister, Rachel Lawson, runs the store with the determination of an iron fist, all the while looking like a goddess that can bring a man to his knees with just one glance. Or so I've been told.

Personally, I've learned not to cross her and everything in our world runs smoothly.

"Sure thing," I say. "Just gather it up and I'll run it out there. Going to walk down to the coffee shop. Want something?"

"The usual. Thanks."

I learned a long time ago that Rachel has her own system and the last thing she wants is me, her older brother interfering in how she does things.

She'd learned to survive the hard way. While I'd been fighting for our country as part of Special Forces, she'd been fighting to keep our family business afloat.

Our father was older and when he'd had to step down, Mother had stepped down with him. Now they both live in a facility that takes care of Father. Having run our family business since she was a teen, Mother practically runs the facility, quietly from the inside, refusing to leave our father.

She gave everything up for Father, with the kind of love you read about in books.

Rachel, with that same family stubbornness, refused to let go of our family business.

I retired early to come back and help her out, but honestly, I'm not sure she really needs my help outside of the heavy lifting and running errands. Granted, that's a big part of our small-town business.

As I step out onto the sidewalk, I check my phone for the time. I'm not just my sister's errand boy. I also fly people in and out of Alpine Falls in my helicopter.

And in less than three hours I have to be in Denver to pick up a couple of guys who are coming out for the weekend.

It's what we do. I get them here and my sister outfits them.

It's how we spend our summers.

My route to the coffee shop takes me past the Amtrak depot.

There are three ways people can get to Alpine Falls.

Drive. Fly. Or come in on the train.

People who can't afford to charter a flight on my helicopter or come in on a small airplane, either come in on the train or they drive.

Most of the people who take the train are just passing through. Sometimes they spend a few hours before taking the next train back to Denver. It is, after all, considered one of the most scenic train routes in the country.

My attention is drawn to a young lady, maybe mid-twenties, standing alone at the depot, flanked by two over-sized suitcases. A leather computer bag weighs heavily on one shoulder.

She looks more like she's moving than coming for a visit. Definitely not just here for the day. Not with all that luggage.

The mountain breeze lifts up her hair and tosses it across her face. As she shoves it back, she scans the area.

I see a familiar wariness in that gaze. The same wariness I often find myself wearing even when I don't have a reason to do so.

She asks the conductor a question, but he just shrugs and walks off.

Asshole.

Every protective instinct I have goes into high gear.

I start striding straight toward her.

But when she sees me, I slow down. Her eyes get big and she actually takes a step backwards.

I don't usually get that kind of response from people. I'm a clean-cut boy-next-door kind of guy. Even being in the military didn't take that away from me.

I approach her slowly, similar to the way I'd approach a stray cat.

"You look like you could use a bit of help," I say.

CHAPTER

FIFTEEN

McKenna

The conductor drops my suitcases off at my feet. *Just doing his job.* No more. No less.

"Do you know if there's a hotel in town?" I ask him.

"Wouldn't know," he says and walks away.

Not helpful.

Since I'd left my cell phone in the river at Casper, Wyoming, I can't very well look it up. I allow myself a moment of envy at other people, all of whom, of course, have their cell phones open.

I'll just have find out the old-fashioned way. Go into town and ask someone else.

I scan the area, looking for any sign of Silas Crowe or his

ilk lurking about. Even knowing that he can't possibly know I'm here doesn't stop me from worrying that he might.

As I stand there, contemplating which way to go, a man in his early-thirties or so strides toward me. A good-looking boy-next-door looking guy, but there's an edge beneath that exterior. Not a bad edge. Just an edge of some sort.

I don't have time to contemplate where that might come from though. He's walking straight toward me with purpose. In fact, if I didn't know better, I'd say he knows who I am.

Not possible.

Nonetheless, without even thinking about it, I take a step backwards.

The man slows and approaches me now with obvious caution.

I grip the handles of my two suitcases and hold my ground.

I don't recognize him. He's handsome, clean-cut. Wearing jeans and work boots. A black leather jacket over a white t-shirt.

He looks nothing... nothing... like Silas Crowe. The complete opposite of Silas Crowe. If Silas Crowe could be flipped backwards and inside out...

I shove my hair out of my face and stand my ground.

Surely he has a good reason for approaching me.

Maybe he's not even approaching me. Maybe he's just

coming to board the train. I am, after all, standing on the depot.

"You look like you could use a bit of help," he says with a little half-grin.

I glance behind me, but there's no one else he could be talking to. Besides, his blue eyes are most definitely pinned on me.

"Do you happen to know if there's a hotel in town?" I ask.

"There's no hotel."

"Oh." No hotel. Perhaps this had been a bad idea. I still have time to get back on the train.

"There's a lodge, though. The Alpine Falls Lodge. And there are a couple of rooms in town that might be available."

"Which do you recommend?" I ask, relieved that I don't have to somehow get my suitcases back on the train.

"I recommend one of the rooms. Closer than the lodge."

"Can you point me in the general direction of one of those rooms?"

"If you'll let me take your luggage, I'll escort you there myself."

I release the handles of my luggage. Couldn't refuse such an offer if I wanted to. "Okay."

He grins and takes a step forward. "May I?"

"Are you a valet?"

He lifts an eyebrow. "At the moment, yes."

"Okay."

He holds out a hand for my computer bag. I happily slide it off my shoulder and hand it to him. He effortlessly settles it on his own shoulder.

Then he takes the handles of both my suitcases, one in each hand and rolls them as though they weigh nothing. I happen to know that they're quite heavy.

"Planning on staying awhile?" he asks.

"I'm hoping to stay somewhere for awhile."

He gives me a little nod to my non-answer to his question.

"Where are you from?" He asks it as though it's a casual question. And being here in a small town, a tourist town from what I'm seeing so far, it's doubtless an almost expected, routine question.

"I'd rather not say."

"Ah. A mysterious lady arrives in town."

He doesn't seem offended, just a bit amused.

"Something like that."

"Well," he says. "Let me be the first to welcome you to Alpine Falls."

I glance around at the little town, my gaze drawn to the tall mountain peaks towering above a town at what I'm guessing is at a high elevation in itself.

I follow him along a stone path that leads us toward the main street. "The air feels different here." I put a hand on my chest. "Lighter."

"We're over nine thousand feet. Have you been up here before?"

"No." I don't elaborate. The less anyone knows the better.

"It can take a little getting used to. You might want to take it slow at first if you're not used to the higher elevations."

"Duly noted."

Reaching Main Street, we turn left.

Main Street consists of a wide two-lane road with parking on either side. Two rows of shops and restaurants.

About half a dozen cars and trucks moving about. But most people are on foot. I'd say there are about twenty people walking along the sidewalks. Coming in and out of shops.

They look like tourists if their brightly colored shopping bags and ice cream cones are any indication.

I follow him into a shop called the Lawson Outfitter's Supply.

There are only two customers in the shop right now. A middle-aged man and woman looking at some fishing poles.

A younger woman, about my age, is explaining something to them about the fishing poles. I hear the words *fly fishing* and *lures.*

The woman looks up at us, after darting a quick glance at me, raises an eyebrow at my escort.

"Just getting the key," he says.

She shrugs and goes back to her customers.

"I'll be right back," he says, leaving my suitcases as he walks into the back.

Not that I have any personal experience with it, but the store looks like it has just about everything needed for camping. Lanterns. A camp stove. Ropes.

There's also an aisle of food. Bread. Chips. Refrigerated items like frozen pizzas and ice cream sandwiches.

And then there's a section of t-shirts, postcards, and other souvenirs like mugs and puzzles.

My escort returns out of the back.

"Need anything?" he asks.

"Maybe later. Is there a room?"

"Yes. You're in luck."

I follow him out of the store, left again, then down another path toward a house set behind the store.

The large two-story house resembles a log cabin, except it's more modern than what I think of when I picture log cabins.

An old-fashioned swing sits on the front porch with pots of flowering plants spilling out of them.

Instead of going in the front door, he leads me around the back of the house.

The back of the house is more impressive than the front.

There's a little rock garden with a bubbling water fountain.

Outdoor furniture. A table with a light blue umbrella in the middle. A fire pit that looks like it's been used quite a bit.

He stops at the back door and inserts a key into the lock. Pushes the door open.

I guess I've been traveling so long, a week, that it doesn't even bother me that I don't know him. I step inside and take a look around.

The little room has a king-sized bed with a white comforter and an extra throw folded across the foot of the bed.

Two large windows overlook the back of the house, both of them with shades rolled high to let in the view and the sunshine.

He places my computer bag on a small table that can be used to either eat or do some work.

I see a bathroom through an open door.

Looks like it has everything a hotel room would have.

"Will this do?" he asks.

"It's perfect," I say. "Do I need to check in somewhere?"

"No," he says. "You can settle up with Rachel later."

"Rachel?"

"The woman you saw in the shop." He doesn't make any moves to leave. Just stands there. Looking at me.

"Okay." I rest a hand on my purse. "Right. I'm supposed to tip you."

He tilts his head to one side, looking momentarily perplexed.

"No tip," he says, glancing at his watch. "I have something I have to do right now. But if you can wait until I get back, I'll buy you dinner."

But I'm supposed to be tipping him... "Okay." I don't know why I agree so readily. Maybe it's because he makes it sounds so simple. So normal. Almost like it's part of the deal.

He carries my luggage. Finds me a room in the back of a house off of Main Street. Buys me dinner.

He lays the key on the table next to my computer bag. "You can let yourself in and out with this key. That door there," he nods toward a door on the other side of the room. "Leads into the main house."

"Oh."

"Don't worry. You can lock it from this side so you have privacy."

I was actually thinking it needed to lock on the other side.

"I've got to run," he says, turning around. "I'll see you for dinner."

I stand there in the middle of the room and watch him walk out the door.

Not only does he not know who I am, I don't even know his name.

CHAPTER
SIXTEEN

CALEB

AFTER I LEAVE the guest room at the back of my house, I head straight to my truck.

Two things occur to me as I back out of the driveway.

One. I never made it to the coffee shop. Rachel will just have to get over it. I don't have time now to get coffee and still make it to the airfield on time.

The second thing that occurs to me is that I've settled a young lady in our guest house and I don't even know her name.

Rachel will have to get over that, too.

I rescued the young lady from what looked like a bad situation and the rest will fall into place.

It takes me twenty minutes to get to the airfield behind the Alpine Falls Lodge where my helicopter sits on a helipad.

Besides the helipad, there is a small runway, used by any small airplane pilots that want to use it. Mostly it's used by Skye Travels, but since most of the people who fly in stay at the lodge, the lodge owners don't complain about anyone using the airfield.

They don't even mind that I keep my helicopter parked there. Today is a case-in-point. I'm heading into Denver to pick up a couple of guys who will stay at their lodge before and after their foray into camping. Most city people prefer the comfort of the lodge, even though they'll venture into the woods for a night or two. Just for the experience.

Frankly, I had plenty of outdoor experience as a kid. I'm just fine with my modern conveniences.

After a manual check of the helicopter, I climb aboard and run down my preflight checklist.

Minutes later, I'm in the air. It helps that I'm the only one who flies the helicopter. It's exactly the way I left it yesterday when I'd gotten back from a flight. Doesn't change the fact that everything has to be checked before and after each flight.

Typically being in the air is where I feel most at home.

I head east, flying through a few wispy white clouds as I gain elevation. Not much wind today, though, making it a perfect day for flying.

I like it that when I'm in the air I have time to think

about nothing. Ironically thinking about nothing is when I solve most of my problems.

Today, though, instead of settling in to just enjoy the flight, I find myself calculating how soon I can be back to Alpine Falls.

I can't stop thinking about the girl I'd rescued at the Amtrak depot.

Rachel will deal with the details. She always does.

She'll probably wonder why I didn't get the girl's name. After she gets over the disappointment that I didn't bring her coffee.

Not a big deal. Rachel and I have been through a lot together and we not only work well together, we understand each other.

She'll understand my need to rescue my unnamed damsel in distress.

She would do the same.

Being part of a community like Alpine Falls and being an integral part of that community, we're accustomed to taking responsibility for people like our new guest.

Whatever distress I saw in her may or may not be well-founded.

Either way, it doesn't matter. The girl was looking for a place to stay and I found one for her. It just so happened to be the home I share with my sister. The same home we grew up in.

The guest room has been occupied by a lot of people

over the years. A grandmother for a few years. Our aunt for awhile until she got married and moved away.

On occasion, we rent it out to a traveler looking for a place to stay. Usually happens when the lodge is full to capacity during Christmastime. A couple of people have stayed there for what most would consider long-term—several months, but most only stay a few days, weeks at the most.

My knee jerk reaction isn't usually to put travelers in the guest house. Usually Rachel is the one to make that decision.

But something about the girl standing at the depot looking vulnerable and lost had me instinctively wanting to take care of her.

It's funny. I can't even remember the last time I went out on a date. There's nobody who lives in Alpine Falls I want to go out with and I avoid tourists. That never ends well considering that I'm more of a relationship guy than a one-night stand kind of guy. Always been that way. Rachel used to rib me about thinking I had to marry a girl if I went on a date with her.

I think I missed my chance back in kindergarten with Mary Beth. Mary Beth and I were planning on getting married. But then her parents moved away before first grade. My first taste of real love has never been matched since.

I grab my two tourists, already down a beer or two, but fortunately they were at the airport early, ready to go, and head back. They do a good job of entertaining themselves, so I'm left to my own thoughts.

It's so not like me to ask a girl out on a date like that. And just as surprising, she agreed to go.

If she's still there when I get back, which I'm not sure I'm counting on, to be honest, we'll go to dinner and that will be that. I'm not sure what kind of tourist she is, but I do know I didn't see a moving van.

No need to get my hopes up that she might be the woman who changes my life. I'm not that out of touch with reality.

SEVENTEEN

McKenna

Even though I need to go in search of Rachel and get myself checked in, I take my time, enjoying the feeling of being somewhere and not feeling like I have to worry about where I'm going to go next.

Since I've decided this is where I'm going to stay for awhile, an impulsive decision if ever there was one, I hang some of my clothes in the closet and put some in the dresser.

Then I run a hot bath and soak for half an hour.

It's such a relaxing feeling knowing that no one knows where I am.

If my family needs to get in touch with me, well... I don't

know what to do about that. I can't worry about them. They're all off doing whatever they want to do, so now it's my turn to do the same.

I'm taking care of myself.

I pour a generous amount of lavender-scented soap that comes with the room into the bath water and it suds up into far more bubbles than I expected.

Nice and relaxed, my mind gets down to business. Whatever had possessed me to agree to go to dinner with the valet?

I'm here trying to keep a low profile. Not make new friends.

But he'd been so helpful and he was undeniably handsome. I guess if I'm honest with myself, I'm feeling a little lonely for a conversation with someone. Just a normal, everyday conversation that doesn't involve why I'm here or what happened to my best friend or why I don't want to go into Witness Protection.

Someone who doesn't look at me with pity. Not that Miles and Tabby did that. Not intentionally anyway, but it was there.

I'm just biding my time, waiting for Silas Crowe to get himself back in prison where he belongs so I can go back to my life as a prosecutor and future judge.

I refuse to think that my career goals are over and done with. I worked too hard for too long to just give up that easily and become a barmaid somewhere.

I'm certain that being a barmaid is a perfectly respectable career, but it's not my career. I'm a future judge.

So I'm just going to hide out here in Alpine Falls, waiting until it's safe for me to go back to Houston.

I'm certain Silas Crowe will do something stupid to get himself tossed in prison where he belongs. Out on a technicality. I don't get it. Miles had helped me with that case, one of my first. We had everything covered.

How did he find a technicality? And who found it for him? His defense attorney retired two years ago.

I think maybe he escaped prison, but Miles said it was a technicality.

As my bath water starts to cool off, I get out and put on a light blue day dress with a white cardigan.

Remembering I have a date, of all things, I dry my hair, straightening it out as I go, and put on some light makeup. Mostly just some sparkly eyeshadow and mascara. Some lip gloss.

It's time for me to go in search of Rachel.

Wearing my purse over my shoulders, I lock up and retrace our earlier steps around to the shop on Main Street. Keeping my purse with me is of utmost importance.

I had the forethought to cash out my bank accounts before I left Houston. Most of my money is in bank money orders payable to myself, but I have a significant amount of cash with me. A money belt for my waist is on my to-find list.

The shop is quiet at the moment. No customers. It

somehow smells like outdoors. Like spruce and rain. Somehow they made the inside of the building smell like the outdoor experience that they're selling.

Rachel, a frown on her face, is sitting behind the counter, tapping on the computer keys.

She must have seen me come in because she doesn't so much as look up as she speaks to me.

"Did my brother get you settled in?"

"Brother?"

"Yes. Caleb." She says it like I'm daft.

"I thought—" Of course he wasn't really a valet. "Yes. Thank you."

Rachel glances at her watch. "He owes me a cup of coffee and he was supposed to make a campground run."

"Oh."

"I can still make the campground run if you'll watch the store until I get back." She looks up then, pinning me with piercing blue eyes that match her brother's. I can definitely see the resemblance.

"You want me to watch the store?" I ask. I have absolutely no experience in retail. None. I didn't work through college or any of that. I was a student. Then an attorney. Nothing in between. The only thing I know how to do is attorney-related.

"Yes," she says. "My customers at the campground have been waiting for an hour."

"Okay," I say. I honestly believe that if I refused to help her, she'd send me packing right here on the spot.

I'm getting the feeling that staying in the room Caleb set me up in comes as a package deal.

Help the sister in the store.

Go on a date with the brother.

So I clamp my mouth shut and don't tell her that I have absolutely no idea how to *watch the store.* Maybe no one will come in. It seems to be pretty quiet.

It strikes me as odd that she trusts me to mind her store while she doesn't even know my name.

Obviously there's been some misunderstanding.

She's assuming that since her brother put me in what I'm getting the feeling is their guest room, that he knows me.

A reasonable person in their right mind would correct that assumption before it goes any further.

I, apparently, am not a person in her right mind.

I just hope I'm never put on the stand and forced to defend my actions.

"Good." She comes from behind the counter, picks up a bundle of fishing poles and tackle and starts toward the door.

"Can I help you with that?" I ask.

"Just get the door," she says.

I hurry ahead of her and hold the door open while she walks through with her arms loaded.

"Call me if you have any questions," she says as she walks off.

"Right."

I go back inside the store.

Call her. How exactly?

All I know is that her name is Rachel. That and she apparently has a brother named Caleb with whom I have a date tonight.

Neither of them know my name. They know absolutely nothing about me.

I walk tentatively behind the counter and sit down on the stool.

Me, a perfect stranger, has just been left in charge of a camping store.

It's so ironic, I almost laugh out loud.

It's a good thing I'm not a thief. I could rob them blind.

To what end, I don't know. The fact remains that I could.

Instead, since that doesn't sound like much fun, I get up and wander the store, familiarizing myself with things. I don't even know what half the stuff in here is for, but there's one thing I do know about myself.

I can learn.

CHAPTER

EIGHTEEN

CALEB

WHEN I LAND, I have a few texts from my sister. Annoyed texts. The annoyance comes through her texts loud and clear.

> RACHEL
>
> I guess you forgot the coffee.
>
> RACHEL
>
> And that you were going to run
> some things to the campground.

Damn it. I certainly did forget to do the campground run.

Rachel has every reason to be upset with me about that.

The coffee, she'll get over. But when it comes to the customers, she takes that seriously.

> Just landed. I'll be right there. I'll run it out to the campground.

RACHEL

> Don't worry. I've got it. Your girlfriend is watching the store.

I stare at the message.

My girlfriend?

She means the girl I put in the guest room. The girl whose name I don't even know.

I am in so much trouble. On so many levels.

I can't even think about how to respond to her right now.

Deciding it's best if I say nothing, I set my phone aside and go through my post flight checklist.

My passengers are already walking toward the lodge, ready to get their adventure started. So my responsibilities are taken care on this end, at least.

Now all I have to do is deal with an irate sister. *All* I have to do. Right.

She thinks the girl I put in the guest room is my girlfriend. I hope she was nice to her.

My sister is a perfectly lovely, friendly person. Until she's crossed. And usually when she's crossed it's because of something having to do with the store.

She takes her stewardship of the store seriously.

And I crossed her when I didn't run the supplies out to the campground. I'm fairly certain she either gave them a hefty discount or comped them altogether. So the customers are happy, but that doesn't make my sister happy.

And then there's my *girlfriend.* With dread eating at my stomach, I lock up the helicopter and climb into my truck.

I have so much explaining to do and I don't even have a good explanation.

It had not been a good idea to leave my new friend, *my girlfriend,* there on her own with my sister.

Rachel may have run her off by now. She left her in charge of the store. I don't know if that's something my alleged girlfriend knows how to do.

I take a deep breath.

Rachel might be upset with me, but she's very responsible. I'm certain she at least took the time to get the young lady's name before she left her in charge of our store.

Right. Just like I took the time to get her name before I left her in our guest house.

I pull onto the main road and head toward town. I'm certain everything will be sorted out in no time.

A few minutes later, I pull into my parking spot at home and go in through the back door of the store.

My heart slams into my chest as I recognize my new friend, my alleged girlfriend, immediately. She's wearing a light blue flowing dress that falls below her knees with a white sweater over her arms. She looks very preppy, in an traditional east coast preppy fashion. One that I've found attractive. Probably because I went to college in Boston.

With her profile to me, I see her hair falling down her back in soft straight waves. Interesting. She'd had it pulled back in a messy ponytail earlier.

She and a young man, a customer, stand in front of our selection of camping stoves. The young man's gaze is glued to her face. From his expression, it wouldn't matter what she's saying. He's obviously more interested in her than he is in whatever stove they're looking at.

"That's a good question," she says. "Let's see what the box says." She turns the box and begins reading highlights from the back of the box.

"Okay." The man leans closer as though he's going to read along with her.

"This one has two adjustable burners," she says. "A removable grate." She glances at him. "Do you have propane?"

He gives her a look as though she might be daft.

I close the distance between us.

"This is actually our best-selling cook stove," I say, taking it from her hands. "I'll ring it up for you. Do you need anything else? Propane?"

"No," the customer says. "I've got everything else. My stove just went out."

"Good." I walk toward the checkout counter, making the bold assumption that he's going to follow. He does. As does she.

I ring him up quickly, take his payment, and get him out. The man is wearing a wedding ring, for God's sake. He should be ashamed of himself.

This is why I don't get involved with tourists.

Once he's out the door, I turn to my alleged girlfriend.

"Hi," I say.

"Hi. Thank you. I don't know anything about cooking stoves. I guess you could tell."

"He didn't care about the cooking stove," I say.

"What do you mean?"

I shake my head. "My sister did this to you."

"It's okay. She had to go out to the… campground."

"I know. I was supposed to go, but I ran behind."

"My fault."

"Not your fault at all." I can't blame her for my forgetfulness. It's not her fault I was in a hurry to go so I could get back here. Even if she's the one I was in a hurry to get back to. "I'm Caleb."

"I'm McKenna," she says, holding out a hand.

"McKenna. It's a pleasure to meet you."

She smiles and bites her bottom lip. "You smell like jet fuel."

"That's a keen observation on your part."

"Have you been to the airport?"

"Something like that."

"I dated a pilot in college." She tilts her head to the side. "You have the look."

"The look, huh? What look is that?"

"The look of a pilot."

"Again. Keen observation on your part."

"So... Are you? A pilot?"

"Helicopter."

"Oh. Impressive. It's my understanding that flying a helicopter is more complicated than flying an airplane."

"I don't know about that. Was my sister nice to you?"

"She was... she wasn't not nice."

"She's a bit funny when it comes to the store."

"She runs it then?"

"It's her store." A young couple walks in through the front door, the ringing bell signaling a customer. "Just hang out here. I'll take care of them."

"Ok." She sits down on the stool, looking quite relieved.

I like the way she looks sitting behind the counter. She looks like she belongs.

But I'm getting ahead of myself.

It's just dinner.

Just dinner.

CHAPTER

NINETEEN

McKenna

I sit on the stool behind the checkout counter and let out a quiet sigh of relief.

Retail looks so easy from the outside. But helping people figure out what to buy is much harder than it looks.

Besides the guy who bought the stove, there had been a customer looking for fishing lures. I admitted I was new here and didn't know anything about fishing. He said he'd come back. Think I lost that sale.

Then there had been the little family who bought t-shirts and a birding book. Everything had gone okay until it was time to check them out. I honestly hope they hadn't seen the fear on my face at the prospect of using the register. Fortunately, since I'd used self-check myself, the scanning part was easy and you can only imagine my relief when his credit card went through and a receipt printed itself out.

I'd felt pretty proud of myself for completing that transaction, even though I hadn't really done anything.

Then there was the stove guy.

Caleb had come to my rescue just in time on that one.

I watch as he talks the young couple through their tent choices. No pressure. Just explains everything and lets them pick out the tent that suits them best.

After he rings them up and they leave, he pulls a stool up and sits next to me.

"I'm sorry my sister put you to work."

"It's okay. It's been interesting."

"You don't know much about camping, do you?"

"Your turn at making a keen observation."

He smiles. "Not hard to figure out. What do you do?"

"I'd rather not say."

"Right." He gives me a little nod. "The mysterious woman from the train."

"It's for your own protection." I twirl around on the bar stool, facing the front of the store. "How far is the campground?"

"About thirty minutes. She should be back anytime."

"Does she work here all day? Seven to seven?"

"Most days, yes."

"No help?"

"You angling for a job?"

I smile. "Maybe. But I don't think I have the qualifications."

"No? I can interview you. Basic stuff. Not getting into your undercover operation."

I swivel back to face him. "Okay."

"How many years have you worked in retail?"

"Zero years. Zero months. Going on two hours now."

"So... no retail experience."

"I would not discount my two hours of on-the-job-training. It was sort of like... boot camp."

"Boot camp? Seriously that bad?" He looks a bit horrified.

"Boot camp in a good way," I say.

"Okay. Where do you see yourself in five years?"

Such an innocent question and we're just playing around. It's not a real interview. We're playing around. Waiting for his sister to come back so we can go to dinner.

But I break out into a cold sweat and a buzzing shoots through my ears.

I twirl around, my back to Caleb, and put a hand on the counter to steady myself.

I honestly feel like I might be going to pass out.

Moments later... I don't know how long... Caleb hands me a wet cloth. "This might help," he says.

With a quick glance in his direction, I take the cool cloth

and press it against my neck. It helps. I dab it against my cheeks and that helps even more.

"Thank you," I say, still not facing him.

Somehow he knew I was having a panic attack. He knew it before I did.

"You're welcome. Are you better now?"

"I think so. How did you—? How—?"

"I was in special forces," he says. "I know a panic attack when I see one."

"Well. It's my first one. So you're one step ahead." He doesn't say anything. "I guess I failed my interview."

"Actually. You passed with flying colors. The job is yours if you want it."

I turn to face him now. "You must be really hard up for help."

"Nah. We have lots of applicants. But most people try to fake their way through the questions. Not you. With you I think I know what I'm getting."

Biting my bottom lip, I shake my head. "Thank you for being kind."

"I only ask one thing in exchange," he says.

"What's that?" I ask, wary now.

"Let me know if there's anything you need. Anything I can do to help."

All it takes is a few kind words for my eyes to well up with unshed tears. I look away, not wanting him to see.

So kind. How is it I stumbled onto someone who's so kind?

"Rachel's back," he says.

"Oh dear." I straighten on the stool. Wonder if I should even be sitting down.

"Give her a chance."

"Okay. But you do realize she's quite frightening, right?"

He just smiles. "Yes."

CHAPTER
TWENTY

Caleb

"Thanks for watching the store," Rachel says as she breezes through the store going straight through into the back room. She barely even looks in our direction.

"You're welcome," McKenna says, but I'm not sure Rachel even hears her.

"If you're back," I say. "We're just going to head out to dinner."

"Go ahead," Rachel calls from the back.

"You ready?" I ask McKenna.

"Sure." McKenna follows me out the front of the store onto Main Street. "I'm a little worried about your sister. I think she really needs some help with the store."

"I give her a break when she asks for it. She really prefers to do things her way."

The sun is dropping over the mountains, reflecting off the forever snow-capped mountain peaks, leaving shadows behind.

"Okay. I don't mean to get into your business. It just seems like she's a little stressed out."

"Be careful," I say. "She'll have you on the payroll."

"I don't think it would be all that bad."

"Careful what you wish for. How does pizza sound?"

"Pizza sounds great."

"It's the Pizzeria or the Hungry Biscuit."

She give me a perplexed look. "What's the Hungry Biscuit?"

"A local chain. They have great hamburgers."

"Pizza sounds good."

"Pizza it is."

Together we walk down Main Street, past the Amtrak station where I'd first seen her.

"Do you like your room?" I ask.

"It's lovely. Very relaxing."

"Good."

"Is that your house it's attached to?"

"It's the house we grew up in and yes. My sister and I live there now."

"Your parents?"

"They live in a facility." I don't like talking about it, but it's no secret. Anybody in Alpine Falls would be more than happy to give her the details. It's best if I tell her. "My father is older and has a type of dementia. My mother gave everything up to go and live with him at a facility in Denver."

"That's so sad and heartwarming at the same time."

"I know. They love each other deeply. I'm not so sure he even remembers who she is, but she's unwavering."

"I'm so sorry," McKenna says. "I shouldn't have asked.

"No. I'm glad you did. I'd rather tell you the truth than have someone else tell you something that may or may not be true."

We reach the pizzeria with big band music spilling out the door.

"It smells wonderful," she says.

"They make good pizza. Brick oven roasted."

We find a booth at the back and sit on opposite sides of the table.

The light blue leather seats have been around for a long time, but they're still comfortable.

The painted stone tiles on the top of the booth, faded and worn, but I can only imagine the conversations they've heard.

A pretty blonde haired girl I recognize as my neighbor's high school daughter comes to the table. Offers us beer.

"Just water for me," McKenna says.

"Two waters. Thanks Abigail."

"What kind of pizza do you like?" I ask McKenna, picking up a menu.

"I'm easy. Anything with cheese."

"You're in the right place. What's your favorite?"

"I like plain cheese."

"Cheese it is. Good choice. They're world-renowned for their cheese pizza."

"Really?"

"No. But it is one of their popular menu items."

"You're funny."

"Thanks." And even though I don't say it, I feel like McKenna needs cheering up.

I noticed her wariness right away when I first saw her at the train station, but the sadness layered over her is even stronger.

Wariness and sadness. And an unwillingness to talk much about herself. Add on the panic attack triggered by a simple question.

Something happened to this girl. Something bad.

And I hope she gives me the chance to help her. Even if it means I just get to distract her for a little while.

TWENTY-ONE

McKenna

Sitting at a booth at the pizza parlor in the small town of Alpine Falls seems so... unexpectedly normal.

I didn't get off the train here in this small town to end up sitting across from a handsome local man. Not by any means whatsoever.

I'd gotten off the train here because the little town had called to me. The air light with the high elevation and the scent of spruce trees had been irresistible.

It had seemed like a safe place. A place hidden away from the world.

Or maybe I had simply been tired of traveling and wanted to simply *be* somewhere.

But I'd stumbled my way into the Lawson family.

They don't know who I am and they don't seem particularly concerned with finding out. At least not yet.

They will. They have to. Especially with me staying in their guest house and minding their store. If I go to work for them, they'll need to do a background check on me.

Then they'll know I'm an attorney and where I'm from.

I square my shoulders. In that case, I can't go to work for them. I can't put them in danger that way.

I play the script through. They find out where I've worked. They call to check references.

Now Miles knows where I am.

Somehow Silas Crowe finds out.

Follows me here.

Put the Lawsons in jeopardy.

I can work for them. Help out in their store. But I can't give them my real last name.

Some people run background checks without permission.

"This is a nice place," I say, having figured out what I need to do or rather not do.

Big band music spills from hidden speakers and all the booths are filled. I don't know if the customers are residents or tourists. Having never been a tourist myself, I don't have that discerning eye. At least not yet.

"I like it. See the older fellow back in the kitchen?"

I follow his gaze. "The one wearing the white chef's hat?"

"Yes. Give him a minute and he'll toss a pizza crust into the air. Turn it into a perfect circle."

Leaning my elbows on the booth, I watch as the man kneads a pizza crust, then sure enough, he tosses it up into the air and effortlessly catches it on the way back down.

"Impressive," I say. "He must have been doing this for a long time."

"Since he was knee-high to a tadpole. Learned at his daddy's feet."

"This place has been here a long time then. It has the feel of it."

Thick stone walls. Time-buffed ceramic tiles on the tabletops. A stone hearth in the kitchen that looks like it's been there a hundred years.

"One of Alpine Falls' finest."

"You're proud to be from here. Have you ever lived anywhere else?"

The server brings our water. Takes our order.

The teenagers in the booth behind our burst into care-free laughter.

"Lived in Boston for some time."

"Boston. Wow. How long?"

"Six years."

"And you came back here." I lean back against the booth and study him. "University."

"Yes."

He has the east coast look about him. Wearing jeans and a preppy white button-down shirt. I attributed his look to him being a pilot, but it also goes with his east coast education.

"I'm officially impressed. Did you always know you'd come back here?"

"I did." He shrugs. "Mostly."

"Mostly says something."

"It doesn't, doesn't it?" He leans back, too, and runs a finger along his glass. "That was about the time our father got sick and Mother left Rachel holding the store. My thinking was to come home and help her. Turns out she doesn't really need it."

"I don't know. I think maybe she needs your help more than she lets on."

"Are you a psychologist?"

"If I was, I couldn't tell you. Right now I'm just a mysterious girl from the train."

"With a quick wit." He lifts his glass in something of a toast and takes a sip of his water.

I watch the pizza chef toss another crust into the air.

"Does he ever miss?" I ask.

"I've never seen him miss."

"Everybody misses," I murmur, but I'm talking about myself now. I missed. I missed keeping Jennie safe. My miss didn't result in something so benign as a pizza crust on the floor though. My miss resulted in the loss of a life.

Miles and Tabby tell me it wasn't my fault. The police tell me it wasn't my fault. I tell myself it wasn't my fault.

And yet I'll never forgive myself.

"Penny for your thoughts," Caleb says.

"Sorry. I drifted away, didn't I?"

"Yes. You did. You can talk to me. It's part of our bargain. You can talk to me about anything. And it stays right here. Between you and me. No one else."

"Thank you." Tears well in my eyes again. He's so kind and I believe his words. But I won't confide in him. I can't. I can't risk putting him or his family in danger.

I've been through that.

And I never want to go through it again.

TWENTY-TWO

Caleb

Abigail drops off our pizza and leaves us with two plates.

I slide a slice of the cheesy pizza over onto one plate and place it in front of McKenna.

I hate seeing the pain in her eyes.

Even though I know telling her that she can confide in me won't make her do it, I mean it when I tell her she can tell me anything. She can tell me anything and it will stay between the two of us.

I can't help but start to imagine what might have happened to her.

The first thing that springs to mind is an abusive

boyfriend. It's always an abusive boyfriend that sends girls into hiding.

And McKenna is definitely in hiding.

I don't think she even realizes how carefully she scans the room, looking for whoever she's hiding from. It seems like it's already become a part of who she is.

I hate that for her. I know what it's like to live with wariness. It's no way to live.

As much as I would like to help her, I know I can't.

If it's not an abusive boyfriend, then maybe she did something to get herself in trouble with the law. I don't quite think that's it, though. She doesn't seem to mind if she's seen. She's just watching for someone in particular.

"So tell me, McKenna," I say, drawing her gaze back to mine. "How long are you planning to stay here in Alpine Falls?"

"I don't know. My plans are undetermined."

"Depends on your undercover operation."

"Yes. I guess it does."

"Well. You can stay in the guest house as long as you want to."

"Rachel might not agree with that. She might have other plans for the guest house."

"She might. I don't think so. But if she does, we'll figure something else out."

"The lodge."

"There's always the lodge. Although it does book up at times. Especially around the holidays."

"That's a long time away."

"It'll be here before you know it."

She nods slowly. Then easily changes the subject. "You studied aviation?"

"I had a double major. Aviation and business. I stayed on and got my MBA while working as a private pilot. Skye Travels offered me a job."

"I've heard of Skye Travels," she says. "It's hard to get on with them, isn't it?"

"It's not easy. But my ability to fly both airplanes and helicopters got Noah Worthington's attention."

"Noah Worthington. Isn't he the owner of Skye Travels?"

"Owner and founder."

"You didn't take it, though, because you came back here."

I slide another slice of pizza onto her plate. "You got it."

"It's what you told me."

"I think you're a psychologist," I say.

"What makes you say that?" she asks with a little smile.

"Because you're a good listener."

"Maybe I just pay attention."

"Maybe. But I think it's more than that."

"I'm not sure I'd make a very good psychologist," she says.

"Why's that?"

"Because I'm not good under pressure."

"There. See. You just told me something about yourself."

She hadn't meant to. I can tell by the expression on her face that she hadn't meant to reveal anything about herself.

"It's okay," I say. "Your secrets are safe with me."

And now I'm ever more convinced that she is actually a psychologist. A psychologist who had something go very wrong for her.

I will convince her that she's safe with me. I don't know how yet, but I will. Maybe it'll just take some time.

TWENTY-THREE

McKenna

Since there are people waiting for a booth, we don't linger long after we've eaten.

When I get back from the restroom, Caleb in signing the credit card receipt.

"When do I get to pay for something?" I ask as we step outside into the cool night air. I'm thankful I wore a sweater over my dress, but I'm wishing I'd worn a jacket.

"Who says you do?"

"I haven't even paid for my room."

"But you worked for free. So far I'd say I still owe you."

I shake my head and glance around the well-lit streets.

The shops are still open, people coming and going. It's an idyllic setting. So serene and safe looking.

And yet I can't help but halfway expect to see Silas Crowe sitting on a bench, wearing his work shirt, watching me. Just like he'd been when he'd sat across the bar watching me.

Waiting patiently for me to let my guard down again.

Only now I picture him with blood on his hands. Just as I'd had blood on my hands when I'd tried to save Jennie.

Caleb is asking me something, but I zoned out again.

"I'm sorry. What's that?"

"How about a game of pool?"

"Pool?"

"Yeah. You know with the cue sticks and the balls."

"It's been awhile since I've played pool."

"But you have played."

"Sure. It's a normal college student pastime."

And I just told him I went to college and played pool.

There's no way I'm going to avoid telling him anything at all about myself.

I just have to focus on two things. Not telling him my real last name and not telling him where I'm from. Those are the two things that will reveal my identity. Everything else is just generic.

"Double or nothing," he says.

"Double what?"

"If I win, I get to take you to dinner again tomorrow."

"And if I win?"

"You get to pick the place." He grins. "You really can't lose here."

"Alright fine. But I should probably warn you."

He holds up a finger. "It's just for fun."

"Okay," I say. I said it had been awhile since I'd played. I didn't say I wasn't any good.

We walk into the pool hall which is more like a family arcade. Teenagers linger over the video games. There's apparently a mini golf out back.

"Does mini golf sound more fun to you?" Caleb asks, seeing me peeking outside at the course.

"Next time," I say. "Right now you've got me set on playing pool."

"Sounds good."

There are two pool tables and surprisingly enough, both of them are available.

"Not too popular?" I ask.

"Comes and goes. We got lucky. Your choice of pool cues."

I pick up one. Balance it in my hands. "This one will do." I've learned that the pool cue doesn't make all that much difference.

"Do you want to break?" he asks, setting up the balls.

"No. You go ahead."

Even though there is absolutely no reason to think that Silas Crowe followed me here, I gaze around, looking for him anyway. Just families here. No reason to be alarmed.

Caleb breaks and balls scatter. One of the solids goes in, but he misses the next shot.

"Your turn," he says.

"Don't take it easy on me," I say.

"Who says I'm taking it easy?"

"Just saying."

"Blue stripe in the side pocket," I say, then proceed to drop the blue striped ball in the side pocket.

"Fancy," Caleb says. "A call shot."

I shrug. "Old habit."

"Okay. Now what?"

"You're implying that was an easy shot."

"Not implying."

"Well. It was. Red stripe in the side pocket."

"I don't think you can—"

The yellow ball slams into the red striped ball, sending it straight into the side pocket as planned.

"You were saying?" I ask with a raised eyebrow.

"I didn't say a word."

"Yellow ball in the far side pocket," I say and proceed to put it there after it bounces off the table wall.

I always feel a little guilty when it comes to playing pool. Almost like I'm cheating. My grandfather had owned a pool hall and since my parents had been working and doing their own things, I'd ended up at the pool hall more days than not after school and more weekends that I could think about.

My grandfather had taught me to play pool and then I

had practiced. This had all been before the doors opened, of course. Grandpa would never let me in the pool hall after it opened. In fact, I was fifteen before he ever let me inside with the public.

I distinctly remember it. I'd sat on a stool and watched a group of boys struggle their way through a game of pool.

I remember thinking. *I could make those shots. I could beat these boys at this game.*

That was my first inkling about just how good I'd gotten at playing.

When I'd asked Grandpa about it, he said. "It's a good skill to keep up your sleeve. It's one of those things you can surprise people with when they least expect it."

He'd been so right about that.

Didn't keep me from feeling like I was cheating.

"Eight ball in the side pocket," I say.

"Guess you'll be picking the restaurant tomorrow," Caleb says, running a hand along his chin. "Where did you learn to play pool?"

I weigh my answer. I don't want to lie, but I don't want to tell him too much either.

"My grandfather had a pool table," I say. He actually had eight pool tables, but close enough.

"Ah. Now that explains things."

"Want to play again?" I ask.

"Sure," he says a bit warily.

"You can go first."

"I don't want you to take it easy on me," he says, mirroring my words.

I laugh. "It's a little late for that. I've already revealed my hand."

Together we pull the balls out and put them in the table.

"Do you want a beer?" he asks.

"Sure. But I have to warn you."

He holds up a hand. "No warnings necessary. I already know you can kick my butt at pool."

Biting my bottom lip, I smile at him.

This had been a good idea.

TWENTY-FOUR

CALEB

MCKENNA'S whole face lights up when she smiles. Her teal green eyes sparkling even more.

I decide right then and there with a pool cue in my hand that I'll do whatever I have to do to make her smile as often as possible.

Even if I do have to let her kick my butt at pool to do it.

Fortunately, I don't have any kind of problem with letting a girl beat me at pool. It's just a game.

I leave her long enough to order us a couple of beers. When I get back, she's sitting on a stool, surveying the room.

I haven't seen her check her phone, not even once. A rather unusual thing these days.

"I'd offer to let you break," I say. "But then I wouldn't get a turn."

"I've been known to miss on occasion," she says, watching me now.

"I don't think that's something I want to put any bets on."

There's a flash of a smile across her face again, but the hauntedness is back in her eyes.

"You know you could run a hustle at this game."

"I could. But that doesn't seem right."

"A pool shark with scruples. I like it."

"I'm not a pool shark," she says.

I set my beer down and break. Two solids go in.

"Good job," she says.

"Just luck, my dear," I say.

She shrugs. "Luck is a huge part of any game."

"Luck is a huge part of life isn't it?" I say, aiming for the blue solid ball.

"Luck and chance."

My blue ball drops into the side pocket.

"You're not a believer in hard work?"

"Oh," she says. "I'm a very firm believer in hard work. Without the hard work to land on, luck and chance would fall flat."

"Like an ember on the snowy ground."

"Yes." She take a sip of her beer. "Good analogy."

"Think I can make that red ball?"

"I'd go for the yellow by way of the green."

I put a hand on my hip. Study the playing field. "I don't think that's possible."

"Sure it is. It's easy."

I look over at her. She means it. "Show me."

"I can't. It's not my turn. And those aren't my balls."

"I invoke you as my proxy. I want to see you do it."

"Okay." Standing up, she hands me her bottle and leans over the table. Without so much as a hitch, she manages to hit the green ball just right, sending the yellow ball into the far pocket.

"Wow. I should have videoed that," I say.

At first she looks pleased, then she has a deer in the headlights look back on her face. She quickly recovers.

"You can't do that, remember? I'm undercover."

"Right. You're right. It was just such an impressive shot."

"Your turn," she says, going back to her seat.

I miss the next shot mostly on purpose in order to get her up and moving again.

Her not wanting to be videoed adds another level to her hiding out. I hadn't said I would post the video, but of course, there is always that possibility anytime anyone is videoed.

She seriously does not want someone to know where she is.

I won't make that mistake again.

"Give me a challenge," she says.

"What?"

"Tell me what ball to go for."

"Okay. Go for the blue striped one."

"Piece of cake," she says, making it look exactly like that.

I study the table, looking for a harder shot. "Can you put that green ball in? I don't think it's possible."

She studies the table. "That would require a whole lot of luck."

"And skill. Can you do it?"

"Let's find out."

TWENTY-FIVE

McKenna

After we finish up our very unconventional game of pool, we head out of the pool hall/arcade back toward the Outpost.

Most shops are closed now and there aren't too many people walking around. Many look like workers heading home after a day of work.

"I can't believe you missed that shot," Caleb said. "And it was so close."

"I warned you I was out of practice."

"Well. Maybe so. But your out of practice and most people's out of practice are entirely different."

I pull my sweater tighter as the cool breeze sweeps over me. "You set me up with an almost impossible shot."

"You did ask for a challenge."

"I did. You're right."

Walking past the Outpost, I see that the doors are locked and the lights are off.

"Do you think your sister has forgiven us yet?" I ask.

"I don't know. She'll be over it by morning though."

"I hope so."

"I don't have a flight tomorrow," I say, glancing at my phone to make sure no one has contacted me.

"That's good. So you'll be helping Rachel out in the store?"

"If she needs anything. Want me to drive you up to the lodge? Show you around?"

"Trying to get me ready to be booted out of the guest room?" I ask.

"Not booting you out," I say, lightly bumping her elbow with mine. "Most people enjoy seeing the historical lodge."

"Okay. Sure. What time?"

"We can have lunch there if you want. Why don't I text you?"

"I don't have a cell phone," I say.

I stop walking and look at her. "I don't think I've ever heard anyone say that before."

"I lost it on the drive. It's no big deal."

"I can't imagine."

"It's okay. I'll be up. I'll come to the store and find you."

"Deal."

We start walking again, leaving Main Street and heading down the path leading to his house.

"You want to come inside?" he asks.

"No. That's okay," I say, thinking about Rachel still being upset. "I think I'm going to get some sleep."

"Okay."

He walks me to the door. Stands aside while I unlock the door.

"Goodnight then," he says as I open the door.

"Goodnight." I turn, standing in the doorway, my hand on the doorknob. "Thank you."

"For what?"

"For letting me win at pool."

"You say that like I had a choice." But he grins, his hands in his pockets. "I'll see you tomorrow."

"See you tomorrow."

I close the door and turn the lock.

The first thing I do is walk around, checking for signs that anyone has been inside the room while I was out. Seeing no evidence that anyone was there, I close all the shades and get ready for bed.

I hadn't expected to have a good time tonight.

In all honestly, I think I hadn't expected to have a good time ever again.

I feel a little guilty at having had a good time after what happened to Jennie. This is the kind of thing I would normally tell her about. How I just happened to stop in a little town and ended up having a good time with a strange man even though I hadn't planned on anything of the sort.

She would laugh at me and tell me that there's nothing wrong with enjoying the company of a handsome, charming man.

I change into my pajamas and realize I'm inclined to agree with her.

I can't remember the last time I spent an evening thinking about something other than work. I just hate the circumstances that got me here.

Sitting on the edge of the bed, I contemplate Caleb's reaction to me not having a cell phone. He's right, of course. It is very odd for someone to not have a cell phone.

There's a landline on the nightstand.

After a moment's hesitation, I pick it up and listen for a dial tone.

Why not? I dial my own number and check my voicemail.

You have ten new messages.

Laying back on the bed, I listen, dreading each one.

Three are spam. Four are from Miles. The other three are routine work messages.

At least no one is looking for me. And I don't count Miles in that.

It's a relief knowing that my family is okay at least.

Either Miles hasn't called them yet or they don't care enough to call and check on me. I hope Miles hasn't called them yet.

I envy Caleb his close connection with his sister. Even if Rachel is scary, she and Caleb are obviously close enough that they live in the same house and work together.

It would have been nice to have been that close to one of my brothers. To at least have been close enough to have one of them check in every now and then.

Workaholism runs in the family. I can't fault them for doing their own thing.

And I could have called them after Jennie. I just hadn't wanted to explain anything to them. Miles had been pushing at me to permanently upend my life with Witness Protection and I had just needed to get away.

Now that I'm away, I have the time for things to sort themselves out without that permanent life change. Once Silas Crowe is back in prison, I can go back to Houston and pick up where I left off without having lost my identity.

Surely everyone will understand.

Surely this won't put a permanent scar on my work record.

I get up and walk around, checking both door locks again. The door that leads outside and the door that leads into the main house. Both are locked.

If it does, it just does.

I can always take up a career in pool hustling.

After I climb into bed, I pick up the phone and check my messages.

You have no new messages.

A little odd. But good, I decide.

Still holding the phone receiver, I waver. It's late. An hour later in Houston than it is here.

Taking a deep breath, I dial the office number. Then hang up before the answering service picks up.

I've got a better idea.

I dial Mile's direct office line.

He won't be there. It's too late.

"This is Miles. Leave your name and number and I'll get back to you as soon as possible."

"Hey Miles. It's McKenna. Hi. I know this is probably weird, but I need a favor. Would you go by my condo and bring my ivy in off the balcony? Take it to your house and look after it? It's kind of sentimental or I wouldn't ask. I'll explain later. Thanks. I'll 'um. I'll talk to you soon."

TWENTY-SIX

SILAS CROWE

SILAS CROWE STANDS in the shadows of Mile's office and looks through every piece of paper he can get his hands on.

After he come up with nothing giving any clues about where to find McKenna Moore, he goes to the computer and hacks in.

That's the thing about prison. You come out knowing more about how to break the law than you knew when you went in.

An hour later, he sits back and glares at around the office. It's clear that the bastard Miles has had no communication with McKenna Moore since that night he ripped the life out of Jennie whatever her name was.

When the office phone rings, he freezes and listens.

He listens as the bitch McKenna's voice comes over the line. Chatters about some plant she left at her condo. Women worry about the stupidest things.

Other than fucking, they're not good for much else. This one, though. This McKenna has it coming back to her. She's the one who sent him to prison. Maybe he'll just fuck her before he smothers the life out of her. Hell, maybe he'll fuck her while he smothers out the life.

The thought gets some action going in his pants.

Leaning forward, he checks the caller id. Recognizes the Colorado area code. Interesting.

Very interesting.

He grabs one of Mile's sticky notes and uses his best pen to write down the number.

Silas prides himself on his level of calmness even in the face of something so monumental as this. So important as finding out, finally where the bitch crawled off to.

He'd been tracking her phone as she zigzagged in true panic fashion across the country. Lost track of her when her phone went dark. Before it went dark though, he learned that she was headed for Oregon.

Looks like she took a little detour.

Very convenient of her.

And to leave her phone number, too.

Very considerate of the little bitch.

TWENTY-SEVEN

CALEB

THE NEXT MORNING, just as dawn is breaking over the mountain peaks, I find my sister in the kitchen.

"Morning," I say, heading for the coffee machine.

"Morning," she says, already sitting at the kitchen table reading the local newspaper. She reads every word of the newspaper every week the day it comes out. It's one of the ways she keeps up with what's going on in town. That and people coming in the store to gossip.

"How was your date?" she asks, not looking up.

"Good. She's a nice girl."

"Last time I checked," she says, glancing briefly at me. "You don't date tourists."

"I'm not sure she's a tourist," I say, sitting down across from her with my own coffee.

"What are you thinking then?" she asks, looking at me now with genuine curiosity.

"Not sure."

"So you don't know who she is or why she's here."

"Her name is McKenna."

Rachel takes a sip of her coffee. Watches a couple of birds fight over the best spot in the bird bath.

"And you put McKenna in our guest house."

"That just about sums it up."

"I see." Rachel taps her phone to read a message that chimed on her phone. "Shipment will be here in twenty," she says, seemingly forgotten about McKenna. But she hasn't.

"I'll head over. Get everything loaded into the stockroom."

"I'll come with you," Rachel says, but makes no move to get up. "You going to marry McKenna?"

"What?" I nearly spit out my coffee. Instead, to keep from spitting it out, I burn my tongue. "Why are you asking that?"

"Because I never see you dating anyone. And you've always had some weird idea that you have to marry every girl you go on a date with."

"It was just dinner," I say, evading the question. "I saw a vulnerable girl at the train station who needed a place to stay. So I helped her out."

"Huh."

"You would have done the same."

Rachel shakes her head. "I don't date girls."

"You know what I mean."

She smiles. "You have any flights today?"

"No. I'm going to help you. And then I'm going to take McKenna out to the lodge for lunch."

Rachel raises an eyebrow. "Sounds serious."

"Okay." I hold out my hands. "You got me."

"You already have the ring?"

"Do not."

"Guess you'll be flying into Denver then."

"I think I'll take her with me and let her pick it out."

"Good idea. Since she's going to be part of the family, you need to teach her about fishing lures and camping stoves."

"How do you know about the camping stove?"

"You think I'd leave a perfect stranger in my store without cameras?"

"No. I don't guess you would. You want me to get us breakfast from the Hungry Biscuit after we get the shipment unloaded?"

"Sure. Might as well bring something for McKenna, too. She can start working the store in between your dates."

"Right." I get up and pour the rest of my coffee down the sink.

It occurs to me that this conversation started by Rachel in jest is feeling far too real.

She's right. I don't date casually and for me to so much as take a girl to dinner is unusual in and of itself.

We could almost be having a real conversation about McKenna.

Almost more than almost.

TWENTY-EIGHT

MᴄKᴇɴɴᴀ

I ɢᴇᴛ ᴜᴘ ᴇᴀʀʟʏ the next morning because it's what I do. I get up early.

Attorneys wear their lack of sleep like badges of honor.

Any attorney who wants to be successful gets up before the sun and burns the midnight oil. Before long, it becomes an ingrained habit.

So I get up. Take a shower and get dressed. Then head out in search of coffee.

Last night I'd seen a coffee shop not far down the street.

I'm unprepared for the cold that hits my skin as I step out the door.

I'm also unprepared for seeing Caleb walking in my

direction, hands in his coat pockets, an enviably heavy wool coat.

"Good morning," he says.

"Hi."

"You're up early."

"New place," I say. It's not untrue.

"I would have texted, but..." He shrugs. "I was coming to ask you if you wanted me to bring you something for breakfast."

I don't bother to tell him that there's a phone on the nightstand. Maybe he doesn't know. Or maybe it's connected to the house's main phone line. It's actually something I need to know. If I'm checking my messages and someone inside the main house picks up...

"You know there's a phone in the guest house."

"Really? I'm not sure I did. Maybe Rachel knows the number."

"It's okay." And a relief. "I was heading out to get coffee."

"Want company?" he asks.

"Sure." I shove my own hands into my jeans pockets, trying not to look at his coat.

"You don't have a coat," he says.

"Didn't bring it."

Without asking, he shrugs out of his own coat and holds it out for me to put on.

"I can't take your coat."

"Of course you can. If people see me walking around in a coat while you're freezing, I'll be cast out as a cad."

"Oh. Well." I settle into the warmth of his coat. "We can't have you being cast out or being called a cad."

"That's right. There's a shop in town that has a coat you might like."

"I could buy one from your shop."

"Nah. Too bulky for you. Not your style."

We turn right and stepping onto the Main Street side-walk, pass the outpost heading the same way we went last night when we walked to dinner.

"And how do you know what my style is?"

"Not hard to figure out."

I look at him from beneath my lashes. "What's my style?"

"You really want me to tell you what I think?"

"Yes. Tell me."

"Okay. I think you're a city girl. College educated. And I think you're from the south."

And he's right on target.

"What gave me away?" I ask, playing along.

"I got the being from the south part from you not having a coat."

"Maybe I forgot it. It is practically summer."

"Only a southern girl would forget her coat. When heading into the mountains. In spring."

"Okay." He makes a good point. "What about the rest?"

"The college girl from the city I've known since I first saw you. It's just woven into everything about you."

Even in the south there are hundreds of cities I could be from. So far he's just touching on generic things.

"That all you got?"

"So far," he says. "But I'll keep you posted. The Hungry Biscuit is down this street."

We make a right. "Does everyone come here for breakfast?" There is a line out the door.

"At some point. Yes. Rachel and I come here just about every other day."

"Because who has time to cook, right?"

"Exactly. You won't find Rachel in the kitchen. Unless she wants to be."

"Sounds like me."

"Not a big fan of cooking?"

"I can do it when I have to."

He smiles and we take our place in line. "You say it like you'd rather eat boiled spinach."

I make a face. "I don't think it's quite that bad. But really. Who has time?"

"I agree. It can be fun though."

"My friend and I used to—" I stop myself in midsentence and look away.

I'd almost told him about when Jennie and I used to cook sometimes and that's not the worst of it. The worst of it is the wave of nostalgia that sweeps over me. I'll never get to spend another evening cooking pasta, her favorite, with Jennie.

He doesn't seem to notice though. He doesn't seem to notice that I nearly broke down right there in front of him.

"I'll get us a table," he says, stepping toward the hostess stand.

"Sure."

What is it about this guy that has me wanting to tell him about everything? I've known him less than twenty-four hours and it seems like I just open my mouth and things spill out. Things I know I shouldn't be talking about.

I have to pull myself together.

CHAPTER
TWENTY-NINE

Caleb

I step away from McKenna to give her time to pull herself together.

For someone who doesn't want to talk about herself, she doesn't do a good job of keeping things to herself.

"Table for two," I say. I was planning on just getting takeout, but since we're here, I figure McKenna and I might as well sit down and eat.

"Where's Rachel?" The hostess, Mandy asks, giving me the stink eye.

"At the shop. I'll get takeout for her."

"See that you do," Mandy says. "Have to watch out for my buddy."

"My sister will not go hungry," I say, feeling the need to defend myself for being here with someone not my sister. It's crazy.

Maybe Rachel was right. She hadn't come right out and said it. But maybe I did need to date more often.

I glance back at McKenna. Not likely to happen now though. Now that I've met McKenna, my one-woman loyalties have kicked in.

I might know better than to think that I'm going to marry McKenna, but it doesn't mean I'm going to be interested in anyone else for a very long time.

It's just the way I'm built.

McKenna is slowly revealing little things about herself at every turn and she doesn't even realize it.

Maybe I'm just good at putting pieces together in a way that makes sense.

I already know that something bad has happened to her and as a result of whatever that was, she's hiding out.

I'm now thinking that whatever that thing was, it has something to do with her friend. I don't know if her friend is male or female. Not yet.

My guess is that something happened to her friend and they aren't friends anymore. So maybe a guy friend.

I may be grasping at straws now, but I'm getting a general framework.

Leaving Mandy, I go back to McKenna.

"You okay?" I ask.

"Uh huh." She glances at me, but keeps her gaze away.

"Remember," I say, leaning close and saying it so only she can hear. "We have a deal."

"I know. I can talk to you anytime about anything."

"You are such a good listener."

"I know."

"Caleb." Mandy calls my name. "Your table is ready."

"I think they were ahead of us," McKenna says with a nod at the group standing in front of us.

"We're getting a small table. Don't worry."

We follow Mandy to a little table for two at the back of the restaurant.

McKenna takes off my coat and hands it to me.

"That's rather nifty," she says, as I hang it next to the table.

"What's that?"

"A coat hanger on the wall next to the table."

I hold her chair as she sits down. "You are so from the south, my dear."

She smiles. "Maybe I just don't get out much."

"Oh. You get out plenty." I sit down across from her.

"Coffee?" Our server asks.

"Just water," McKenna says.

"Thought you were headed out for coffee," I say.

"No offense but I think I'll hold out for the coffee shop."

"Not a bad idea. I'll have water, too."

"Coming right up, Mr. Caleb."

"You know everyone," McKenna says.

"It's a small town. Everybody knows everybody."

"They must all be talking about you then."

"Why's that?"

"Because they don't know me."

"Probably. The hostess all but scolded me about making sure I get Rachel something to go. I almost felt like I had to defend myself for being with you."

"Funny. We'll get her something. Right?"

"Absolutely. Wouldn't dare go back emptyhanded." I hand her a menu. "Are you a big breakfast eater?"

"I can go either way. Sometimes I skip it altogether and just have coffee."

"Part of the being undercover life."

"It's hard work."

There's a hint of that smile I've been looking for.

"Maybe you'll tell me about it sometime."

"Maybe."

CHAPTER
THIRTY

McKenna

If I'm not careful, Caleb is going to know everything about me whether I intend to tell him or not.

It seems like things just keep slipping out at every turn.

After we place our order, the server leaves us alone.

The restaurant is different from what I expected. The chairs are covered in worn red vinyl and we're seated near a window with a view of the mountains.

The mountains look like they're just right there, but, of course, they aren't. Ruggedly tall and snow-capped, they have a layer of wispy white clouds hanging around them.

There's no background music. Just the sound of conversations swirling. Silverware scraping against china.

We're sitting close enough to the kitchen to hear the sizzle of the grill behind us. The cha-ching of the cash register as people pay for their food. There seem to be as many to-go orders as there are dine in patrons. Maybe more.

The most unusual thing, really, is the human-sized cardboard hamburger just inside the door, cheerful and absurd in the best small-town way. It welcomes people to come inside and enjoy themselves.

A tall fellow in dark sun glasses walks in with his seeing-eye dog and the hostess sits him at a little table next to us. The dog sits at his feet.

"How are you doing Don?" Caleb greets him.

"That you, Caleb?" the man asks.

Caleb gets up and clasps him on the shoulder. "It's me. Haven't seen you lately. How's it going Nester?" He holds out a hand for the dog to sniff, but doesn't touch him.

"Oh. I've been busy. They've got me teaching online classes now."

"You don't say."

"Yeah. I don't mind though. Is that Rachel?"

"This is my friend McKenna," Caleb says.

"Hello McKenna," Don says, looking in my general direction behind dark sun glasses.

McKenna looks at me with uncertainty, but quickly turns her attention to Don.

"It's nice to meet you Don."

"Well. Enjoy your breakfast."

"You too."

Minutes later, our food arrives.

"This is good," I say, taking a bite of crispy bacon.

"The Hungry Biscuit is known for more than just their biscuits."

"It appears to be more of an atmosphere than just a restaurant. It feels... welcoming."

"Yeah. I think it's a good representation of Alpine Falls in general. It's a chain now. They're popping up in all the small towns around here. Alpine Falls. Even Glenwood Springs has one. But this was the first one."

I have no idea where these places are he's talking about, so I just smile and scoop up a bite of eggs. "Well. I can see why it's successful."

"What do you have planned for today?" he asks.

"I'm supposed to have lunch out at the lodge. We'll see. And then I think I'm having dinner somewhere in town. Maybe here. I don't really know what the choices are. But I have a win to cash in."

Smiling, he leans back in his chair. "Has anybody ever told you that you're delightful?"

"No. I don't think they have."

"Well. You are."

Don, sitting within earshot, clears his throat. "Make sure I get an invitation."

"Hush up now Don," Caleb says.

Don just laughs.

There's an inside joke here somewhere. I just don't know what it is.

They've had a lifetime of living in a small town. Even if I moved here permanently, I'll always be an outsider.

THIRTY-ONE

CALEB

MANDY HAS Rachel's to-go order ready by the time I've paid for our food. She's still giving me the stink eye, but it's not as bad as it was.

She'll just have to get over it. I actually think it's rather weird. I know she knows that Rachel is my sister and surely she knows I'm allowed to have breakfast with someone not related to me.

There are occasions like this when I actually miss the anonymity of Boston.

"Do you want to go ahead?" McKenna asks. "I want to stop by the coffee shop."

"I'm getting coffee, too," I say.

"Rachel's food."

"It'll be okay. I'll get her a coffee. She'll be happy."

"Alright."

We step into the coffee shop and get in line. The scent of dark brewed coffee blends with vanilla and milk. The familiar roar of the coffee grinder and the hiss of the steaming wand punctuate the background hum of machines.

Hushed conversations are interrupted by the barista calling out orders and names as orders are readied for pickup.

It's a universal environment that is replicated all over the country. I can't count how many hours I spent studying in a café just like this, but on the other side of the country.

McKenna orders a latte and I order Rachel's usual cappuccino and a cold brew for myself.

McKenna makes a face. "Cold coffee? On purpose?"

"Only if it's on purpose. Otherwise it's just cold coffee."

"That's what everyone says who drinks it."

"Sounds like you have a lot of experience with people who drink cold brew coffee."

"Caleb," the barista says, sliding my cold brew over in my direction.

"It has one advantage. I get my order quicker."

"That is an advantage," she agrees. "If you're in a hurry."

"I don't know too many women who drink cold brew coffee."

"I don't either."

"So you work with a lot of guys?"

"No. No," she says. "You're trying to get me to talk about my undercover work. Not going to happen."

I take a sip of my cold brew. "Can't blame a guy for trying, now can you?"

"McKenna." The barista slides a hot coffee across the counter. "Rachel's will be right up."

McKenna grabs up her coffee and takes a sip. "Now this is good coffee."

"Some of the best."

"Your friend, Don," McKenna says. "Has he always been blind?"

"No. Something happened when he was a teen. I'm not sure what and it seems rude to ask."

"Oh. So he can't see anything?"

"Shadows. I'm told."

"He's such a brave man."

"You know," I say, leaning back against the counter. "Speaking of Don. I don't know your last name."

"And I'm not going to tell you." McKenna looks at me with big teal green eyes over the coffee cup. "What does that have to do with Don?"

"Nothing. Just makes it hard to introduce you is all."

In that moment, I don't care if I ever know what her last name is.

As long as I get to be near her.

"No one will notice."

"People notice everything."

"They'll get over it."

"Maybe I'll just have to assign you a last name then," I say.

"Assign me one?" she asks on a bubble of laughter.

"Yes. Since you're one of us now, I dub you McKenna Lawson."

Her eyes widen, but she doesn't say a word.

Hiding my grin behind my coffee cup, I shrug.

She's like one of the sirens of lore, luring me over the deadly rocks with her eyes. And I go willingly. Not only willingly, but I'll rip away everything and anything holding me from her just to get to her.

THIRTY-TWO

McKenna

We leave the coffee shop, Caleb carrying not only the takeout bag, but also both cups of coffee. His and Rachel's.

"I can carry one of those cups," I offer for the third time.

"I've got it."

"You've got some kind of thing going on with the manly thing?" Even though I'm asking him this, I don't really believe it. I'm just asking to distract myself from the last name he just gave me. Lawson. I wouldn't tell him my last name, so he gave me his.

It's very disconcerting.

Not that I didn't ask for it. I did. By refusing to tell him my last name.

"I do not have a manly thing," he says. "A small-town man is supposed to be chivalrous."

"Okay," I say. "I just need to feel like I'm needed, you know."

"So you're the one with the thing going on."

I roll my eyes at him.

He hands me Rachel's cup. "Don't say I didn't try to protect you," he says.

"What do you mean?"

"I'm just saying... if you drop it..."

I thrust the cup back into his hand, making sure he has a good grip on it before I let go. "You could have handed me yours."

"If you're carrying mine, how can I drink it?"

"Good point." I turn my face up to the sun. "How is it so cold with the sunshine so warm?"

"It's the magic of Alpine Falls."

I turn and study him. "You really do love it here, don't you?"

"Ah. It's okay."

"I think you do. I think you love it here, but you don't want to admit it."

"Do you love wherever it is you're from?"

The question unsettles me a bit. Do I? I thought I did.

"Of course," I say. "Doesn't everyone?"

"No. Some of my classmates couldn't wait until the ink dried on their diplomas to get out of here."

"Yeah. I can see that. I get wanting the excitement of the big city. Feeling like the small town is holding you back."

"Are you from a small town then? Originally?"

"No. But I've known people who were."

"Right. In your work as a psychologist."

We cross the street, heading to the Outpost.

"Have you ever thought about becoming a fiction writer?"

"Nah. Too much work."

"You're a funny guy." Since his hands are full, I open the front door to the Outpost.

No customers. "I don't see Rachel."

"She'll be in the back."

We find her in her office. A small room with only one window looking out toward the main house. She's sitting behind a desk, her fingers flying over the computer keyboard.

There's a large iPad on one corner of her desk with four camera views of the store.

"Good," she says. "I'm starved."

"Your friend Mandy was a little upset that you weren't with us."

"Mandy at the Hungry Biscuit?" She takes her coffee and tastes it.

"Yes." Caleb pulls her plate out of the to-go bag and sets it on the table.

"That's a little strange."

"I thought so, too. We saw Don."

"How is Don? I haven't seen him in ages."

"He looked good." He turns to me. "Rachel dated Don. Before he lost his sight."

"Really? That must be weird for you," I say to Rachel.

Rachel makes a face. "Dating is a strong word. We were twelve."

Keeping a straight face. "People start dating young here in Alpine Falls."

Rachel and Caleb both look at me as though I've gone daft.

"Just kidding," I say.

"Right." Rachel opens the lid on her to-go plate and starts eating.

I glance at Caleb, wondering how I've somehow managed to offend Rachel again.

"So," Rachel says. "Caleb is going to teach you about fishing lures today so you don't lose any more customers.

I wince. "I'm so sorry about that."

"It's okay. He came back and I helped him. But we get a lot of questions about the lures."

"I would think so."

"Go on," she says with a wave of her hand. "No time like the present."

"We've been dismissed," Caleb says. "And put to work."

Caleb hadn't been kidding when he said Rachel took everything about the Outpost seriously. I'd take that a step further and say that Rachel takes everything seriously.

She's more serious than any of the attorneys I work with.

I'm thinking it would do her some good to get back together with Don. Maybe he could make her lighten up a bit. Maybe even laugh now and then.

"Sorry about Rachel being so cross," Caleb says.

"I guess you're used to it."

"I won't say I'm used to it," Caleb says. "I'd say I've come to accept it and I guess expect it."

"Is Don married?" I ask as we walk toward the fishing lures section.

"Don? Nah. I don't think he ever got over Rachel."

"I see."

Not my business. I'm only here until Silas Crowe goes back to prison and I can go back to Houston.

Rachel and Don are not my business.

Learning about these fishing lures, apparently, though is.

THIRTY-THREE

Caleb

"Let's start with the basics," I say, pulling half a dozen lures from the display and taking them back to the counter. Laying them out strategically.

"Have a seat," I say, going around the counter and indicating one of the stools for McKenna to sit on while I sit on the other.

"Alright. Here we go. Every lure is like a person you meet. They've all got their own personality. Their own method of drawing attention."

"Okay. This should be interesting." She clasps her hands together in her lap and waits for me to explain.

I hold up a shiny spinner. "This one's the spinnerbait. Flashy, loud, impossible to ignore. It's like the person who walks into a room and immediately has everyone looking their way. Fun to watch, but not always who you want to stick with. A lot of times the fish will stand back and just watch it."

Next, I pick up a delicate fly, its feathered wings fine as silk. Handmade by a local man. "This is a fly. Looks fragile, but it's clever. A perfect imitation. That's the person who's good at pretending, at putting on a show. They get noticed fast, but there's not much substance underneath. Fish will take a bite, but there's not much to sink their teeth into."

"I know people like that."

"Haven't we all. Now this one's a crankbait." I hold up a lure shaped like a little fish. "It wobbles like it's struggling, drawing fish to it. It's like the person who thrives on drama. Always reeling you into their messes."

"Okay. But the fish go for it."

"A lot of times, yes. It can be a very effective bait. Quite popular around here."

Lastly, I point to a plain soft plastic worm. "And this little fellow might not be much to look at. No sparkle. No feathers. No drama. But steady. Reliable. When nothing else works, this is the one you count on. Might take patience, but it's the one that lands the fish."

"So which one do I recommend to customers?"

"Depends on what they're after. If they want attention,

recommend the spinnerbait. If they're out to impress people more than actually bringing home the fish." I tap the delicate handwoven fly. "Lead them toward this one."

"If they're serious about catching fish, they need a crankbait or a worm," she says.

"You're a quick learner."

"You're a good teacher." McKenna asks, picking up the soft worm. "Which one of these are you?"

I take a deep breath. "I guess I'm a worm."

"Maybe we need a better name for it." She sets the lure back down.

"I'm open to suggestion."

"How about a classic?"

"A classic?" I say picking up the worm. "I think that fits pretty well."

"Which one of these would I be?"

"You're none of these," I say. "You're a custom-made, one-of-a-kind lure that only comes around once in a lifetime."

"No pressure there," she says, looking away, but I don't miss the light flush on her cheeks.

I grin. "None intended."

"Right. So what else do I need to know?"

"Fly rods. Line weights. Reels. To name a few."

"Okay." She hops off her stool. "Show me."

The little bell over the door rings. "Looks like you're getting your first customer."

"Just throwing me in the deep end, huh?"

"I'm right here." I stand up and follow her out onto the floor.

Turns out she's a natural. Experience or no.

THIRTY-FOUR

McKenna

My first customer, a tourist only here for a couple of days, went for a handmade fly.

I think he wanted the bait more to take home and show off than he wanted it for actual fishing. Either way, he left the shop happy with his find.

"We get a lot of that," Caleb says, showing me where to enter the sale into a separate ledger they keep for the guy who makes the fishing lures.

"You sell a lot of them for him?"

"Every day. From what I hear, most of his sales comes from his website. He has quite the business going for himself. Stays busy."

"Are they all different?"

"No. He makes a few specialty lures, but mostly he churns out his bestsellers in the most popular colors."

"An artist," she says. "But a businessman, too."

"He's an interesting guy. Used to be a college professor. Retired from that now. His wife is a romance writer. I'll introduce you the next time he comes in."

"I'd like that."

Taking a seat on the stool behind the counter and opening a bottle of water, I realize I'm getting to know a lot of people in Alpine Falls.

I've not only met the Lawsons, but I've met Don, the blind guy. Mandy, the cranky waitress. And now I'm learning about the local fly tyer.

I'm also learning about the outfitter's trade, something I never thought I'd have any reason to know anything about.

I've never been camping or fishing or anything related to the outdoors in my entire life.

"It's time to head out to the lodge for lunch," Caleb says. "While we're there, we can try your hand at fishing."

"Fishing? I don't think I'm ready for that."

"We'll start off easy. With a rod and reel. Fly fishing is an art in itself. Something we'll have to work up to."

"I'm not sure Rachel is going to pay me for going fishing."

"On the contrary. You need stories of your own to tell the customers. Makes you more authentic."

"I guess that would be important to Rachel," I say, securing my purse over my shoulder.

"You bet. It's important to everyone around here."

"Right." While I wait for him to tell Rachel we're heading out, I realize I'm feeling like something of a fraud. I don't know how long I'm going to be here.

As soon as I hear that Silas Crowe is back in prison, I'm heading back to Houston to resume my law career.

Caleb is spending a lot of his precious time teaching me things that in my real life I have absolutely no reason to know about.

I can only imagine what kind of strange looks I would get if I started explaining about the different types of fishing lures to people I know in Houston.

And now Caleb wants to take me fishing. Fishing is so outside of my comfort zone, I can't even begin to think about it.

"But first," he says coming out of the back, Rachel right behind him. "I think we need to get you a coat."

"It looks warm outside."

He glances at his phone. "It is warm right now, but that's the thing about weather at this elevation. It can change without warning."

"Sounds ominous."

"Not really. Just have to be prepared." He grabs his keys and coat and we head out back to his truck.

"Okay then. Shopping. Then lunch. Then fishing."

"You left out the best part. The tour of the historic lodge."

"That part was understood."

"You're very diplomatic. Anyone ever tell you that?"

"I might have been told something like that before." It actually fits with my long-term goal of being a judge. I've often been told that have a good sense of impartiality.

"Well," he says, opening the passenger door to his truck for me to climb inside. "It fits you."

"Thank you." I climb inside and settle onto the leather seat of the truck with its new car smell.

Hanging out with Caleb is something I'm getting used to far too quickly.

He gets into the driver's seat and turns on the motor. "Buckle up," he says.

I put on my seatbelt and settle back in my seat.

"It's so pretty here," I say as he pulls out onto Main Street and turn left. "When do I get to go up in the helicopter?"

"You want to fly in the helicopter?" he asks, surprise in his voice.

"Sure. Who wouldn't?"

"A lot of people."

"Because?" Although I've never ridden in a helicopter, I see them all the time on the Houston skyline. Used for various things like emergency transportation and following breaking news.

"Some people find helicopter travel to be a bit rougher than airplane travel."

"But the views." I glance up toward the tall rugged mountain peaks as we leave the city limits. "I would think the views would be more than worth it."

"You're a girl after my heart."

A pleasant flush settles over me.

"And you're a man with a charming tongue."

He just grins. "Can't help it if it's true."

I keep my eyes straight ahead on the road, as we wind our way up the mountainside.

There's something different about Caleb Lawson. Not sure what it is yet, but he makes my stomach flutter with butterflies. And that's something that hasn't happened to me in a very long time.

He turns left down a little two-lane black-top road beneath a canopy of maple tree limbs.

And when I get my first look at the Alpine Falls Lodge, I am quite simply in awe.

It's a two-story log mansion with a wide second-floor balcony scattered with half a dozen little tables and chairs with pretty red umbrellas for shade from the bright sun. Along with the tables and chairs, there are several chaises and from here I see three fire pits sending slivers of smoke curling up toward the blue sky.

CHAPTER
THIRTY-FIVE

"Wow," McKenna says as the lodge comes into view. "It looks like a castle."

"It is rather impressive. It's a popular place for honeymoons."

"And weddings," she says. "It would be a beautiful place for a wedding."

I don't know that they have very many weddings at the lodge, but maybe that's something they should look into. I'll have to ask Rachel.

I pull up into the little parking lot off to the side and put the truck in park.

"The second floor balcony surrounds the whole lodge?" she asks.

I nod.

"I bet the views from up there are amazing."

"Let's go see," I say.

"We can go up there?"

"Sure. I know someone," I add at her quizzical glance. "I'll come around. Get the door."

It's hard to explain how inordinately pleased I am that she likes the lodge.

It guess the lodge represents Alpine Falls in so many way. We had our senior prom here. I've been to several of their Christmas Eve masquerade balls.

I know the owners. The Flynns. Christopher Flynn, also a helicopter pilot, and I were friends growing up. He's married now to an adorable woman named Tabitha. They have a sweet little family. Three children. And from my perspective looking in, he has everything a man could want in life.

Opening the truck door, I hold out a hand to help McKenna out. "Welcome to the Alpine Falls Lodge."

Taking my hand, she slides out. "The air feels different here," she says. "Lighter. And it smells like..." She closes her eyes. "Spruce trees."

"It's about a thousand feet higher in elevation than the town," I explain, closing the truck door behind her. "And the blue spruce trees are everywhere. You can't tell, but it probably just rained."

"It rained?"

"It rains every afternoon. Just a little shower. But it leaves everything smelling fresh and clean."

"If you can't find me one day," she says with a smile. "I'll be up here."

"I knew it. I never should have brought you up here."

"You should have known I'd be enchanted."

"I didn't quite know what to expect." I'm still holding her hand and she doesn't try to pull away.

I accept that it feels natural to be holding her hand.

As we near the front door, the valet opens and holds the door for us.

"Welcome back, Mr. Caleb," he says.

"Thank you, Mitchell. How's the family?"

"All good. Thanks for asking. The daughter leaves for college this fall though."

"Sorry to hear that. But give her a chance. A lot of us come back."

"Gives me hope," Mitchell says. "Take care now."

We step into the magnificent lobby. A big four-sided fireplace is its main feature with several people sitting around the warm fire, reading, using their phones. Talking.

One of the lodge's hallmark qualities has always been its cozy warmth.

"I don't think I've ever seen such a big fireplace," McKenna says. "And real wood. How do they do keep it going?"

"They have a forestry business, too. Plant two trees for every one they cut down. It's very green."

"Impressive."

"Hi Caleb," Zoe sits behind the front desk on the far side of the lobby.

"Hi Zoe. How's everything?"

"Busy. Good." She sweeps the hair out of her eyes.

"This is McKenna." I almost say Lawson, but remember the small town we're in. Conclusions would be drawn and gossip would ensue. Things would never be quite the same again.

"Hi McKenna. I'm Zoe."

"Hi."

I squeeze McKenna's hand.

"Are you here for lunch?" Zoe asks.

"Yeah. Hoping to eat on the balcony."

"It's a beautiful day for it. Go on up. I'll send Antonio up to take your order."

"Come on," I say. "Let's head up and check out the view."

McKenna follows me back across the lobby to the sweeping staircase.

"Wait until you see this place at Christmas," I say. "They always have a tree that reaches the ceiling."

"Seriously?" She looks up. "How?"

"I don't know. Alpine Falls Christmas magic."

"It definitely feels magical and it's not even Christmas."

The lodge has always held a certain magic for me, but right now, it's holding her hand that has that magic magnified a hundred times over.

THIRTY-SIX

McKenna

Out on the balcony around the back of the lodge and up on the roof level, a private area separate from the balcony that surrounds the second floor, we find an empty table with a red umbrella sprouting out of the middle of it and sit side by side in heavy wooden chairs.

Even though there were several guests on the second floor of the balcony, we're the only ones up here. It's not a very big area. Big enough for six tables of four with plenty of space between them.

A light breeze sweeps my hair into my face and I push it back.

"We forgot something," Caleb says.

"What's that?"

"We forgot to get you a coat."

"It's okay. As long as we're in the sunshine, it's not cold."

"Good."

A young man wearing black slacks and a white shirt jogs up the stairs and stops at our table.

"Good afternoon," he says with a decidedly Hispanic accent. "My name is Antonio and I'll be taking care of you for lunch today. Would you like to start with a mimosa?"

"Sure." Caleb looks at me. "Would you like a mimosa? They're quite good."

"Sure. Why not."

"Two mimosas then." Antonio hands us both menus. "Take your time. Enjoy the lovely view. I'll be right back with your drinks."

"No one else is eating up here," I say after Antonio is heading back down the stairs.

"It's not officially part of the restaurant," Caleb says. "They added on this balcony just over a year ago. They only serve food by special request."

"So we're getting special treatment."

"Nothing wrong with a little special treatment now and then, is there?"

"No. I don't mind. And this is really nice."

"They use it for events mostly, I think."

A teenager comes up and lights a fire in the firepit.

"I did that one summer," I say.

"What's that?"

"Worked here as a fireplace boy."

"Really?" She smiles.

"This part wasn't here, of course. My job was to monitor the fire in the lobby. Keep it going. Clean it out ever so often."

"That explains why you like it here so much. Your first job."

"My only job outside of the family store. I was working at the Outpost by the time I could walk good."

"What kind of job does a toddler do exactly?"

"Toddle around and look cute."

"I guess that falls underneath the purview of Child Labor Laws."

"I guess it must. No one ever questioned my parents about it."

"Small towns tend to overlook certain legalities."

"What about you?" I ask. "Did you work as a teenager?"

"Me? No. I was all about studying. I never held a part-time job."

"That sounds almost un-American."

"It does, doesn't it?"

"I always thought working part-time was a right-of-passage for teenagers."

"It is. My parents wanted me to focus on school. So that's what I did."

"You must have done really well in school."

"I did okay." She shrugs. "Top in my... graduate class."

"Graduate class?" I ask. "In psychology?"

She hides a laugh behind her hand. "I can't tell you that."

"Right. I almost forgot. You're here undercover."

"That's right."

"There are so many questions I want to ask you about that," I say.

I know she's not really undercover. But I want to know the real reason she's here. I so much want to know everything about her.

Antonio shows back up then with our mimosas.

"Here you are. Beautiful mimosas for a lovely day at the Alpine Falls Lodge. Would you like to hear our specials for the day?"

"You have specials?" I ask.

"We certainly do. Our new chef is introducing new recipes all the time."

"Well, then, yes. Of course. Let's hear them."

While Antonio rattles off the specials, McKenna gives him her undivided attention and I give her mine.

THIRTY-SEVEN

McKenna

It's a little hard to listen to what Antonio is saying with Caleb watching me so intently.

I pretend not to notice.

"The lobster and shrimp sounds good," I say after he finishes rattling off the specials.

"Agreed," Caleb says.

"So two lobster and shrimp dishes?" Antonio asks. We both nod. "The chef will be delighted. How are your mimosas?"

"We're about to find out," Caleb says.

"Can I get you anything else?" Antonio asks.

"I think we'll be okay for a few minutes."

After he leaves, I lean forward. "Are the waiters always this attentive here?"

"No. Antonio is new and I guess he's just overzealous."

"Yes. He's overzealous. That's the word." I take a sip of my drink. "But this mimosa makes up for it. It's really good."

Caleb tries his. "They have the best mimosas."

I lean back and look out across the meadow that leads down toward the river rushing below. If I close my eyes, I can hear the water rushing over the rocks, but I'm not sure if it's my imagination or if it's really the river I'm hearing.

I open my eyes and freeze.

There are two men standing on the lawn below us.

The one standing with his back to us is holding a pair of clipping shears. The other one isn't holding anything.

But they are both wearing dark green work shirts. The kind that button down the front and have something, probably Alpine Falls, embroidered over the pocket.

The man facing us is looking this way. I'm not sure if he's looking right at me, but it looks like he is.

My blood runs cold and in this very instant, I'm no longer here sitting in an idyllic setting with a handsome charming man. Cool air. Warm sunshine. The scent of spruce trees filling the air.

No. I'm back in Houston. In a little bar below my condo.

Sitting at a table, looking across the room, past where Jennie is dancing with her new boyfriend.

And Silas Crowe is looking right at me. Taunting me. Thinking evil thoughts and planning evil deeds.

I not only forget where I am and who I'm with. I forget to breath.

"McKenna." I hear someone calling my name. "McKenna."

I jump when someone puts his hand on mine.

"McKenna. Are you okay?"

I turn and look into Caleb's concerned eyes.

"I don't know. I—." I look back down at the two men below. The one with the clippers is trimming hedges. The other one is picking up the clippings with his hands. Putting them in a wheelbarrow. He's not looking at me.

And he looks nothing like Silas Crowe.

"Yes." The word barely comes out on a breath. "I'm okay."

But I'm not.

I'm not okay. My heart is pounding and my blood is racing through my veins.

"What did you see?" Caleb asks. He sounds ready to pounce on whatever demon, real or imagined, that I might be dealing with.

I'm not really in a place to tell him so right now, but I appreciate that. That genuine concern in his voice means everything to me.

Unfortunately, it means so much that unbidden tears spring to my eyes.

I've never felt so very alone.

"Hey," Caleb says, scooting his chair close and putting an arm around me. "What just happened?"

I glance quickly back at the men below, still working. "Nothing. I just..." I rub my temples. Breathe in. Breathe out. Breathe in. Breathe out. "I thought I saw..." I shake my head.

"It's okay," Caleb says. "You don't have to talk about it."

I nod.

"Look at me," he says.

I look into his deep blue eyes. A blue that rivals the blue of the endless sky.

His gaze holds mine and doesn't let go.

"You're safe," he says softly.

I'll never know how he knew to say that to me in this moment... how he knew that was what I needed to hear, but he did.

Breathe in. Breathe out.

He sweeps his thumb lightly over my cheek and tucks my hair back. His gaze never leaving mine.

Safe.

And with him here sitting next to me, I don't feel alone.

I feel safe.

THIRTY-EIGHT

CALEB

"This shrimp and lobster is one of the best things they've ever had on the menu and that's saying a lot."

"It tastes like five-star restaurant food," McKenna says with a little smile.

Now and then her gaze darts to the lawn below, but after drinking about half her mimosa, she seems much more steady and relaxed.

Gone now, there were two workers down there, clipping hedges and cleaning up. That's all I saw.

If someone else walked by, I didn't see them. Not saying there wasn't someone else down there. I was watching McKenna. Nothing else.

She'd been visibly shaken. Worse than the panic attack she'd had before. This had been much worse.

I want to ask her about it. I want her to talk about it. But instead I try to distract her. The good food helps.

"You eat at a lot of five-star restaurants?" I ask, not expecting her to answer.

"Sometimes," she says, surprising me.

Of course, that doesn't give me any information about where she's from. There are five-star restaurants all over the world.

Antonio dashes back up the stairs. "Is everything good?" he asks.

"Everything is wonderful," I say.

"Can I get you anything else? Put in an order for apple pie?"

McKenna quickly shakes her head.

"It's very good apple pie," Antonio insists with a grin.

"I can't," McKenna places a hand on her stomach. "This food is so good."

"I will give your compliments to the chef."

"Thank you, Antonio," I say.

"Nothing else then?"

I look questioningly at McKenna.

"I'm good. Really."

"Thank you for dining with us," Antonio says. "We hope to see you again soon."

Then he's off again, back down the stairs.

"Staying in shape is a nice perk of his job," I say.

"I'm thinking I might have to move in here."

I laugh. "I guess they could accommodate that. At the least, they have cabins within walking distance."

"Really? That's interesting to know."

"Bringing you here was definitely a mistake."

She glances toward the distant mountain peaks before smiling into my eyes. "Definitely not. I'm glad you did."

"Are you sure?" I ask.

"I'm sorry about earlier," she says, looking away and swallowing thickly. "I have something I'm dealing with."

"I suspected as much. Remember our deal."

"I can talk to you about anything. Anytime."

"That's right."

"But I don't have to talk about it," she says, folding her napkin and placing it next to her plate.

I can't tell if she's saying that to me or if she's saying it to herself. I decide it's a little bit of both.

"Want to walk around the lodge? Check out the rest of the views?"

"Don't we have to wait for the check?"

"No. They'll send it to the shop."

"Oh. So this is a business lunch?" There is obvious disappointment in her voice. No way to mistake it for anything else.

"Not even close. It's just an arrangement we have with the lodge. When they need something from the shop, we do the same. We just send them an invoice."

"I see. That makes good business sense."

"Come on," I say, "Let's walk around."

I can't figure out why she's so disappointed that I didn't pay for the meal. Why she's concerned that it might be a business lunch. I'm teaching her things about the shop... fishing... and so on, so technically I could make a case for it being a business lunch. The truth is, though, it's just the way we do things.

So I put it aside for now and focus on showing her around the lodge with its magnificent views.

And even more importantly, keeping her from thinking about whatever it is she's going through. At least she admitted to me that she's dealing with something.

We're making progress. Definite progress.

THIRTY-NINE

McKenna

BACK IN THE TRUCK, heading down the mountain toward town, I relax.

Lunch had been wonderful. The views had been spectacular.

But I'd had a terrible flashback.

I'd seen the man wearing the work shirt and it had triggered something visceral inside me. It had taken me back to that night I'd seen Silas Crowe and he had somehow gotten into my home and killed Jennie.

I would never get over that.

And knowing that he's out there cuts me to the quick and leaves me feeling vulnerable.

That simply seeing a man wearing a work shirt can send me back to that night is so disturbing in and of itself. That I'd been with Caleb and Caleb had known what was going on while I'd been struggling with it is mortifying.

As much as I might need to talk about what happened with someone, I just as much don't want anyone to know.

Back to wanting to protect. Jennie had known about Silas and he had killed her. He'd killed her even though I had tried to protect her.

I'll always wonder if he went to my condo expecting to find me and just so happened to find Jennie there. So he'd killed her instead.

She'd been at my condo, a place I'd thought was absolutely safe. Doormen. Concierge. Key fobs for the elevators. Not to mention my condo being locked and no access from outside.

But he'd gotten inside anyway. He'd gotten in and he'd gotten out undetected.

I would never forgive myself for that, even though it wasn't my fault.

He'd killed someone close to me.

And that makes my being close to anyone else a danger to them.

If he finds me.

There's no guarantee he won't find me. Not even with the precautions I've taken.

Caleb pulls off the road and parks in a little parking area next to the river.

"Ready to try your hand at fishing?" he asks.

Fishing. My emotions are feeling raw at the moment. I'd be pushing myself. Maybe a little too much.

"I don't think so. I don't think I'm feeling up to it right now."

He nods. "Okay. But if you'll walk with me, there's something I'd like to show you."

"Okay. I can do that."

I wait while he comes around and opens the door. Like he'd done at the lodge, he takes my hand to help me out and doesn't let go.

As much as I tell myself it's not safe for me to get close to him. That if Silas somehow found me, Caleb would be in danger because of me. Even telling myself that, holding his hand makes me feel safe. Even with the drunken butterflies crashing around in my stomach.

The truth is I like him.

And I'm letting that like override my caution.

Having that flashback at lunch... thinking I'd seen Silas looking up at me... that had been sobering. And terrifying.

We walk a trail that follows along the riverbank. The rushing water is almost too loud to talk over and the breeze carries little splashes of water in our direction, but it evaporates before it hits us.

Even in this peaceful setting, I'm at war with myself.

The trail veers away from the river for a few steps and things get comparatively quiet.

It's like the quiet opens up a pathway in my mind.

A duty to warn.

Tarasoff duty to warn.

I stop right there on the trail as something I learned in law school comes flashing back into my head. Caleb keeps referring to me as a psychologist and oddly enough, this memory comes out of the psychological field.

A duty to warn. I have a duty to warn him about Silas Crowe.

I'm not a psychologist, but the concept is the same to my way of thinking.

He stops, too, and looks back at me, but doesn't let go of my hand.

"I have to tell you something," I say.

It's something that might change the way he looks at me. He would have every right to want me out of his guest house. If not for his own safety, then for the safety of his sister.

I wouldn't fault him for that. I would, in fact, respect that decision.

"Being with me could be putting you in danger."

"How could you possibly be putting me in danger?" he asks, taking a step back towards me, putting him right in front of me.

He's tall. A full head taller than I am and I hadn't even realized it until now with him standing this close to me.

I shift so that I'm looking up into his eyes.

"Something happened," I say.

"I know."

"How do you know?"

He narrows his eyes and I know exactly how he knows. He's seen me have two panic attacks now and he's not blind. He knows that something happened. He just doesn't know what.

"Of course you know," I say. "I told you. But you don't know how bad it is." I bite my bottom lip and rip my gaze from his.

Still holding my hand, he grips my elbow with his other hand. "McKenna. Are you in danger?"

"Yes," I say, my gaze drawn back to his. "Maybe."

He looks over my shoulder. "Has someone hurt you, my dear?"

"No. Not me. But..."

Now that I've started to tell him... to warn him... I don't know how to tell him what happened.

I don't how to tell him without making things worse.

I tug at my hand, but he doesn't let go. "You might not be safe around me."

"I can take care of myself," he says in uncertain terms. I don't doubt that. But...

I shake my head and look away. "No. No one is safe."

"McKenna. I can't help you if you don't tell me what's happened."

I can't tell him.

I can't not tell him.

My thoughts are tangled and I can't think straight.

"He killed her."

"Who killed her?" he asks.

"I can't tell you. Telling you makes it worse."

He takes a deep breath. Lets it out slowly.

"Who did he kill?"

"He killed her. My best friend." A knot is forming in my throat. I can't talk about Jennie. Not like this.

"Who? Who killed her?"

Duty to warn.

"Silas Crowe." The name tastes foul on my tongue. I never want to speak it again. Ever.

"This man. He threatened you?"

"Yes. He threatened me, but he killed Jennie."

"I'm so sorry that happened."

"I shouldn't be telling you this." The words spill out, running together. "Now I have to leave. I can't stay here. Not when he could find me. Not when he could hurt you. You or Rachel."

"No one is going to hurt us," he says. "I won't let him."

"You can't stop him. No one can. It's not safe."

I tug my hand free of his, turn around and start walking.

With tears clouding my eyes, I can't see where I'm going. I don't even know where I'm going. I'm out here in the woods. On a trail. Walking away from the only person who can get me back to town.

I have to get back to town. I have to pack up. I have to go.

It's not safe.

But Caleb is right behind me. I hear his footsteps right behind me.

"McKenna wait. Let me help you."

I stop. Squeeze my eyes tightly.

When I open them, he's standing in front of me.

"Let's go back to town. Find somewhere to sit. Then I think you need to tell me everything. From the beginning."

"Yes. Let's go back."

If I can just get back to town, I can pack my things and get back on the train.

I can leave here. I can leave, knowing that Caleb and his sister will be safe.

If Silas finds me... no one I care about is safe.

He made that perfectly clear.

More than perfectly clear.

He made it real.

The blood.

I can smell the blood. Jennie's blood. Feel it on my hands.

I think I'm going to be sick. Or faint. Maybe both.

Caleb puts a hand under my knees and picks me up. Carries me to bench a few feet up ahead. With no other choice, I put my arms around his neck and after a moment's hesitation, I bury my face against his shoulder.

He sits down, holding me in his lap.

His arms holding me tightly, he rocks me gently.

I don't even realize I'm crying until I feel the dampness of his shirt beneath my cheek.

"I'm sorry," I say and swallow, trying to swallow the tears. But it just makes it all worse.

I'm sobbing now. Sobbing like I never did. Not even after what happened to Jennie.

It's like I'd been holding it all in and now, in this moment, it all comes out. I can't stop crying.

I'm crying so hard I'm trembling.

And I can barely catch my breath.

But Caleb is here. Caleb is holding me. Caleb is gently rubbing my back. Making little soothing sounds.

I've never cried so hard in my entire life. My whole world is crashing in around me.

I don't hear the river rushing behind us. I don't hear the birds in the trees above us or the gentle breeze in the leaves.

I only feel. The loss of my best friend since childhood.

The loss of my own sense of safety. The loss of my own dreams.

The loss of my innocence.

But Caleb is here.

And with Caleb, in spite of everything, I feel safe.

FORTY

Caleb

I HOLD McKenna for what seems like hours, rubbing her back, soothing her.

Hoping against hope that she can catch her breath each time the sobs overcome her.

I'd wanted to show her the river, its peacefulness as the water crashes over the rocks, pooling between the boulders.

There's a little bridge up ahead, not far, that I wanted to show her, but we didn't make it that far before she decided she needed to blindly walk away from me.

Something about keeping me safe.

Doesn't she know that I'd put my own life above hers to keep her safe?

How could she know that?

When she's said something happened to her. When I'd figured out that something happened to her, I'd thought maybe an abusive boyfriend.

I had not thought about someone threatening her and killing her best friend, Jennie.

A man named Silas Crowe killed Jennie and threatened McKenna.

That's why she's here. That's who she's hiding from.

That's why she doesn't feel safe. That's why she doesn't think I'm safe. That anyone she gets close to is safe.

It's a lot. It's not everything, but it's enough for me to know the level of seriousness in what she's dealing with.

And yet all I can do is sit here and hold her while her world falls apart. Sure. It didn't just happen right now, but it may as well have.

She's just now dealing with it. In this moment.

It's as good as just now happening for McKenna.

This explains so much.

It explains why she doesn't have a cell phone. Cell phones can be tracked.

It explains why she arrived on the train. No car.

It explains why she refuses to tell me where she's from.

Everything. It explains everything.

Hopefully it explains enough that I can figure out how to help her.

The first thing I have to do is to increase the security around the guest house.

Correction.

The first thing I'm going to have to do is to move her into the main house.

I can't have her staying in the guest house alone. Even if it is connected to the main house.

No. She needs to be in the main house. In one of the upstairs rooms.

We'll need to get with the sheriff, Bradley Winslow, and have her give a description of this Silas Crowe. We'll put that description out there for everyone to be on the lookout.

If that bastard comes into town, we'll know it.

They can take him back where he came from. Put him back under whatever rock he crawled out from under. He'll be arrested and thrown into prison where he'll never see the light of day again.

Finally, McKenna's breathing steadies and her tears slow.

"I'm so sorry," she says, but it only sends her into another round of sobs.

"You've got to stop apologizing," I says. "It's making you cry."

I think I feel what might pass as a whisper of a smile against my shoulder.

I gently massage the back of her neck.

"I'm okay now," she murmurs.

"Are you sure?"

"I think so, but I think your shirt might be forever ruined."

"This old thing." I don't tell her I'd worn a brand new shirt for the occasion of our day together.

"It smells new," she says.

"There's more where this one came from," I say, still holding her close. Still gently massaging the back of her neck. Still swaying gently with her in my arms.

"I'll buy you another one."

"You'll do no such thing."

"You can't say I didn't try."

"No. I can't say that."

"I could stay right here forever," she says, taking a ragged breath. "It smells so wonderful. With the spruce trees and the river."

"For a minute I thought it was me that had you wanting to stay here forever."

Definitely a smile now.

"Now that you mention it, I'll give you all day to stop with the massage."

"All day it is then. Rachel doesn't need us back at the store."

She lifts her head, concern all over her face. "Is Rachel waiting for us to come back?"

"No," I say with a little smile, looking into her moist green eyes.

Her face is red, but in a good way and her lashes are still moist from crying.

I kiss one eyelid. Then the other.

"I must look a sight," she says.

"You look beautiful," I say.

"My friend... Jennie... always managed to look pretty when she cried."

"Like I said. You're beautiful. And don't ever let anyone tell you any different."

"You're kind."

"I call it like I see it." And even with her eyes puffy and her cheeks streaked with tears, I've never seen a more beautiful woman.

She licks her bottom lip and that's my undoing.

Shifting just inches, our breath mingles together. Another fraction of an inch and my lips press lightly against hers.

She leans forward, kissing me back.

We hold this way as the wind ruffles the leaves in the trees above us. As a wolf howls somewhere in the distance, reminding me that nightfall comes early in the mountains.

"I told you too much," she says, leaning back just a little more than I would like. Just enough to take her lips away from mine.

"Never," I say. "Just a few sketchy details here and there. You've left me to piece things together. And I have to warn you I have a very vivid imagination."

"I don't know about that," she says. "But you have an uncanny ability to put pieces together even when you don't have all the pieces."

"I do, don't I?"

"Yes." She leans forward, placing her lips against mine again.

And I would give her all day to stop doing that. All day long to stop kissing.

I'll give her all day long and the rest of eternity.

CHAPTER

FORTY-ONE

After climbing back into the truck, I pull the mirror down for a quick peek while Caleb walks around to climb into the driver's seat.

All I can say is he must be a blind man to not see how awful I look after my crying jag.

I always envied Jennie's ability to not only cry on demand, but also to look beautiful while doing it.

I've never been able to cry on demand and it's just as well that I can't because the whole point of crying on demand is to look good while doing it, right?

"So here's what I'm thinking," Caleb says. "First of all,

I'm moving you into the main house. We have an alarm system that we don't usually activate, but we will."

"Okay." I don't tell him that it won't help. That Silas Crowe got past concierge and valet and up an elevator that requires a coded key fob before somehow getting into my kitchen. Not to mention out again.

"Second, we'll go see Sheriff Bradley Winslow. He'll get a description of the guy. His sister-in-law helps him out with sketches. We'll make copies and give them to every single person in town. The man won't set foot in town without someone knowing it."

"I don't want my name in the system. I think he might have a way of tracking me."

"How? No cell phone and no car."

"I don't know. I'm probably just being paranoid."

"No." He reaches over and squeezes my hand just before we pull out onto the main highway heading back into town. "You have to go with your gut on these things."

"Then I can't tell the sheriff my last name."

"We'll use your alias. Remember?"

"Lawson," I say, feeling heat rise to my cheeks. "My identification won't match."

"It's okay. We'll figure something out."

As we near the city limits, I turn to him. "Thank you."

"You don't have to thank me."

"But I do. Thank you for letting me have a meltdown on your shoulder. I've never done that before."

"It had to come out. It's better not to keep that stuff bottled up. Or so they say. You would know."

"You still think I'm a psychologist," I say. "I think I'm going to let you believe that for awhile."

"I knew I was right."

"Didn't say you were right. Just going to let you believe it."

"Same difference."

"You're a little stubborn."

"I like to think of it as being determined."

"Same difference."

He laughs and pulls into the driveway.

Before turning off the motor, he pauses and looks at me. "Going to have to tell Rachel. She needs to know how serious the situation is. Needs to understand why I'm moving you into the main house and why we're going to start using the alarm system."

"Okay."

"Anything you want to add?"

"Not really, no."

"Okay. Anything you want me to leave out?"

"All of it. I'd like to leave all of it out. For it to have never happened."

"I'm sure, my dear."

"I think you can tell her what I told you, whatever it was."

"It was enough."

"I was a mess."

He reaches over. Tucks a strand of hair back off my face. "Still a mess," he says.

"Thanks. You have no idea how much that means to me."

"I have a pretty good idea. Look. I won't tell her anything until you're with me. Don't want to get it wrong. Do you want to take a few minutes to freshen up? Pack? Anything? Or do you want to get it over with? Tell her now?"

"Sounds like I need to freshen up."

"Not prescribing. Just asking."

"It's okay. I appreciate the honesty."

"So do I, my dear."

I take a deep ragged breath. "I'm going to freshen up. Take a minute to pull myself together. Then I'll come out to the store."

"Sounds good." But he doesn't turn the motor off. "McKenna?"

"Yes?"

He shifts in his seat, turning to face me more. Waits until my gaze meets him. "I need you to promise me something."

"Okay."

"I know your knee jerk reaction was to run again."

I close my eyes. "I can't deny it."

"Will you promise me that you won't do that? That you won't run?"

I open my eyes and search his. "Yes."

"I mean it. I would hate to have to tear this state... this country... apart looking for a girl named McKenna."

I smile. Just a little. But it's enough.

"I won't run."

"If you change your mind. If you decide to run. Tell me first. Okay?"

"Wouldn't that defeat the purpose?" I ask.

"Depends on the purpose, doesn't it?"

I nod, still studying him. Still searching his eyes for something. I'm not sure what I'm looking for and I'm not sure I'd know it if I found it.

"I think we have something here," he says. "Something worth holding onto." He puts a hand on mine. "Will you give me a chance?"

I think he's asking me to give him a chance to help me. If he's asking me more, I'm not in a place to hear it. Not right now.

"I'll give you a chance," I say.

I really have no choice. It's already been made for me.

It was made for me when he kissed me.

FORTY-TWO

CALEB

AFTER WALKING McKenna to the guest room, I walk around to the main house and change into a sweatshirt.

I might have to tell my sister some of what's going on with McKenna, but I don't have to explain her emotional state.

That's McKenna's business. And, I guess, mine on some level, but mostly hers.

I'm just here to support her as she makes her way through it.

I grab a cold bottle of water from the refrigerator and stand at the window, looking out toward the shop.

When my grandparents built this house, they didn't care anything about having a view of Main Street. It would have been nice if they had. Instead, they have a view of the back of the store. I think they were most concerned about being able to walk back and forth from the house to the store than they were anything else. They put everything into that store.

That's where Rachel gets it. That focused determination.

What they got right was the view from the back of the house. The one looking out toward the mountains.

When it's quiet, mostly at night, with a window left open just a little, I can hear the rushing water of the river from my bedroom.

Having the store between the house and Main Street actually helps cut out any noise from the streets. So maybe my grandparents were onto something after all.

Standing at the window now, processing everything McKenna told me, I'm looking at things a little bit differently.

There are advantages and disadvantages of being off the main street. The advantage is that not too many people know the house is back here. People have to have a reason to know. Mostly delivery people.

The disadvantage is we don't have the added possible eyes on. Being back here, being isolated, allows more opportunity to break into the house without anyone seeing.

I pull out my phone and call the security service to set up a time to come out and check the system. We haven't used it in so long, I want to make sure everything is in top shape.

The soonest they can come out is in two days. Not ideal, but better than I was expecting.

With that done, I head out to the store to wait for McKenna.

"Hey," Rachel says as I walk past her office.

"Hey."

"Thought you were going fishing."

"Something came up and we had to postpone it. No customers?" I glance at the monitors.

"Game night. It's okay. I'm getting a lot of paperwork done."

I know she doesn't mean that. She hates slow days. She'd much rather have steady busy days and burn the midnight oil to catch up on paperwork.

But I'd forgotten that there's a high school baseball game tonight.

"What's up with the positive attitude?" I ask.

"I don't know what you mean." She puts her fingers back on the keyboard and her eyes back on her computer monitor.

I narrow my eyes at her, but whatever it is, she's not ready to tell me.

"McKenna and I need to talk to you," I say.

"You already set a date?"

"A what?"

"A date. For the wedding."

I make a face at her. "I would prefer it be something that simple," I say.

"Okay. Sure." Something in my expression must have clued her in to how serious this is. "We can sit down in the breakroom. Or do you want me to close up so we can go to the house?"

"The breakroom should be okay." I glance at my watch. "Actually. You know what. That's a good idea. We need to walk down and get McKenna a coat. Why don't we do that, then meet in the living room?"

"Okay," she says. "I'll close up early and meet you there."

"No rush. There she is now."

Looking at the monitors, I see McKenna walk in through the front door and stop.

I head out of my sister's office, meeting her in the store.

"Hey," I say.

"Hey. Do I look more presentable now?"

"You look beautiful. Slight change of plans. We're going to get you that coat. Then meet Rachel back at home."

"Okay." She lets out what sounds like a sigh of relief. "I'm not looking forward to this conversation."

We step outside and turn right, heading downtown.

"Any particular reason why?"

"Rachel would have every justification in wanting me out of her house."

"It's my house, too. And I think you're selling her short."

"I don't know." She puts her hands in her jeans pockets and keeps her eyes straight ahead. "She would have every right. No one wants that kind of chaos brought into their lives."

"Rachel is very protective toward people she cares about."

"Exactly," she says, looking into my eyes.

"She knows I care about you, so that counts in her book."

"We'll see."

I take her hand. "You're trembling."

"I know. I'm just feeling off-balance. Talking about... all that stuff... makes it seem all the more real. You know? Dealing with it by myself is easier in some ways."

"And harder, I would think."

"Not sure I know the answer to that just yet." She bites her bottom lip.

I squeeze her hand. "Everything is going to be okay. You've got to trust me."

"It's not about trusting you. It's about what other people might do."

And by other people, I know she's talking about Silas Crowe.

"There's the shop up ahead. I think you'll find a coat there you'll like."

"Okay."

I just need to keep her focused on something positive. Keep her from thinking about the unthinkable thing that happened to her friend.

At least for a little while.

CHAPTER
FORTY-THREE

Caleb and I step into a little shop that smells like cinnamon and vanilla.

I'm not going to find a coat here. I can already tell. I was better off buying a heavy, puffy parka at the Outpost.

This looks like the kind of place old ladies shop. Lots of loose dresses with flowers printed on them. Nothing at all like anything I would wear.

"I can just get a coat at the Outpost," I tell Caleb.

"We'll save that as a last resort."

I take a deep breath. It's not a big deal. It's just a coat.

I don't see any other customers in the shop. In fact, there weren't a lot of people on the streets.

"There isn't a lot of traffic today," I say.

"There's a baseball game tonight," he tells me. "The whole town practically shuts down."

"Caleb," A trim, conservatively dressed Chinese woman with her hair in an elegant updo, appears out of the back. "I was just coming out to close up. No customers tonight."

"It's baseball night, Mrs. Chan." Caleb says.

"Yes. I almost forget. Not big like football."

"No. But they're playing our rival team, Whiskey Springs."

"Yes." The Chinese woman smiles at me. "Hello," she says.

"Hi."

"You came to get something for pretty lady?" Mrs. Chan asks.

"It's okay," I say. "I don't think you have..."

"Do you happen to have a wool coat?" Caleb asks her. "The kind you would wear?"

"A coat. Of course. I be right back."

"I don't think she has anything," I whisper to Caleb.

"I thought you trusted me."

I run a hand along a row of flowered dressed. "One has nothing to do with the other."

He smiles.

Mrs. Chan returns from the back with a solid black wool overcoat.

"This should be your size," she says, removing the coat

from its hanger and holding it up for me to slip my arms into.

With a glance at Caleb, I shrug into the coat while she holds it.

"Look in mirror," Mrs. Chan says, indicating the three-way mirror.

I walk over and stand on the little dais in front of the mirror.

The wool coat looks absolutely like nothing else in the store. It looks like an urban coat. The kind I would actually wear. Solid black wool overcoat with black leather trim at the pockets and the collar.

"It's perfect," I say, turning around to face them.

"We'll take it," Caleb says. "And get out of your hair."

"I send you invoice," she says. "You should go to base-ball game. Wear your new coat."

"Maybe we will," Caleb says.

"I need to pay her," I say as Caleb herds me toward the door.

"You come back if you need anything else," Mrs. Chan says as we near the front door.

"Does she have like a magic room back there?" I ask, as we pass a display of frilly scarves.

"Something like that. She keeps things for the locals. The tourists like to come here and buy things they can't get anywhere else."

"Things they wouldn't wear anywhere else either."

"Probably. But they enjoy it while they're here. Have you never been on a vacation?"

"No. I've never traveled anywhere. Until now."

We stand on the sidewalk outside the little shop. An older couple, obviously not interested in high school baseball, cross the street in front of us.

"This does not count as travel."

"What does it count as?"

"I'm not sure yet."

Music drifts from somewhere.

"Is that a band?" I ask.

"The baseball game."

"I didn't know bands played at baseball games."

"Oh sure. It's quite the production."

"Do you usually go?" I ask, looking at him now.

"Usually, yes. It's good for business."

"I don't want to keep you from going."

"We'll stop by there later. Right now Rachel is waiting for us."

"Right." I glance around at the almost empty streets. I like the town better when there are crowds of people on the streets.

It's a little unsettling being deserted like this, with only a few people walking around, us included.

"The coat looks great on you," he says, taking my hand again as we wait for an vintage pickup truck to pass by, cross the street, and head back toward the Outpost.

"I admit I was pleasantly surprised."

"You just have to trust me on these things."

"You're right. It's your town. You would know."

"And somewhere you have a town… a city… of your own."

"I'm not ready to tell you where I'm from," I say, shoving my left hand in my warm coat pocket. "I didn't pay her for the coat."

"She said she'd send an invoice."

"I know. But. Then I guess I have to pay you."

"You've got to stop worrying about paying for things."

"That's how it works where I'm from," I say. "We get things and we pay for them. Before we walk away with them."

"Such a concept. Maybe we should look into it."

He grins at me and I realize that somehow, someway, despite everything, I'm smiling back at him.

This has to be a good sign.

One that makes me cautiously optimistic that maybe, just maybe, I can one day have a normal life again.

FORTY-FOUR

CALEB

"DID I LEAVE ANYTHING OUT?" I ask McKenna after I finish telling Rachel everything I know about what happened to her.

McKenna shakes her head. She looks quite like she might be going to be sick. I should put an arm around her or at the least hold her hand, but not in front of Rachel. Not yet.

I then look to Rachel who hasn't said a word since we sat down. Very uncharacteristic of my sister to not say anything through this whole recounting.

McKenna watches Rachel warily.

"I can go," McKenna says. "I completely understand you not wanting this kind of danger brought to your doorstep."

"Are you kidding me?" Rachel asks. "No son-of-a-bitch is going to determine who stays in my house." She turns to me. "Put her in your bedroom."

"I was thinking the room next to mine."

"No," Rachel says. "There's a sofa in your bedroom. You sleep on it."

"So... you're suggesting we sleep in the same room."

"What better way to keep you both safe."

"What about you?" I ask, remembering how Silas Crowe had killed McKenna's innocent friend. "We can move another small bed in there. Then we'll all be in the same room."

I'm speaking in jest, but it's not the worst idea.

"My door locks. I'll be fine."

"I don't want to put the two of you through this," McKenna says.

Rachel looks pointedly at her.

"My brother likes you. As far as I'm concerned, that brings you into our family fold."

I hear her unspoken words. *For as long as it lasts.* But she doesn't say it out loud. And Rachel knows me. She knows I don't lightly bring someone into the family.

McKenna's eyes well up with unshed tears, but she doesn't cry. She bites her bottom lip and nods once. I wish I knew what she was thinking. McKenna doesn't share of lot of what's going on with her and yet, from what I'd seen earlier today, her emotions run deep.

Rachel leans forward toward McKenna. "If that man so much as steps on our property, he won't walk out of here. Do you get my meaning?"

"Yes." McKenna lifts her chin. I sense an understanding running between the two women.

Rachel's phone chimes and a glimmer of a smile crosses her features as she glances at the text.

"Now," Rachel says, clasping her hands together in her lap. "I've been craving pizza all day. Anybody want to walk to the pizzeria with me?"

I glance at McKenna. "I could eat pizza. You?"

"Sure."

McKenna is still wearing her coat which I find a little amusing, considering how skeptical she was that she'd like anything that came from Mrs. Chan's shop. Of course, how would she know that Mrs. Chan keeps a private stash for the locals?

Rachel and I get into our coats and three of us head back out onto the nearly deserted sidewalk.

I take McKenna's hand. There's only so much restraint a man can tolerate, even around his sister.

"I'm surprised you didn't go to the baseball game," I say to Rachel.

"Back at you."

"Busy day," I say, squeezing McKenna's hand.

"We can swing by later," Rachel says, echoing what I said earlier.

"I'm curious to see what it's about," McKenna says.

"We'll make it a point to stop by there," I tell her.

Rachel glances at her phone again and speeds up her pace.

McKenna looks at me questioningly. I shrug.

My sister is one of those people who is a mystery to all who know her. Even me, her own brother.

"I hope you don't mind pizza again," I tell McKenna.

"How could I?" she asks.

I smile and lean over to kiss the top of her head.

I can't help but wonder how this most beautiful and delightful woman just randomly walked into my life.

FORTY-FIVE

McKenna

THE ALPINE FALLS PIZZERIA is starting to feel quite familiar. I hear big band music spilling out the door one block over.

Oddly enough, because of the baseball game, it's not as crowded tonight. Only about half the tables are filled.

After hanging our coats on the hooks next to the booth, we sit, Caleb and me on one side. Rachel on the other. With its faded stone tiles, this table has a mountain scene painted in shades of sunset pinks.

We're no more than settled into our seats when our server, Abigail, stops at the table.

"Hi Caleb. Rachel." She smiles at me. "Welcome back McKenna."

"Thanks," I say.

"I'll get you some water and breadsticks right out," she says as she hands each of us a menu.

"She knows my name?" I ask after Abigail walks off.

"It's a small town," I say. "People talk. Anyone moving here is new and interesting.

Moving here. I'm not sure I exactly said I was moving-moving here. Maybe some things are assumed like when someone hangs out with locals. Maybe that changes the whole perspective.

Another server drops an oven roasted pizza off at the table behind us and my stomach growls in anticipation. Seems like we just ate lunch not too long ago. I guess having an emotional breakdown uses a lot of energy.

Still. I get the small town thing and I get that people talk. It's a good thing I haven't told anyone my last name. If I had, I have little doubt that it would be all over town, too.

And having my name all over town makes it just that much easier for Silas Crowe to find me.

"What kind of pizza do you like?" Rachel asks, looking at me, catching me a little off-guard. It's such a normal question and she asks it in such a normal way.

"I'm easy," I say.

"What's your preference?" she asks, sounding back to her typical exasperatedness and pinning me with her gaze.

"Cheese," I say, clearing my throat.

Apparently Rachel doesn't prescribe to the going along

with the crowd mentality. She expects people to have pref-
erences.

The door opens and she instantly looks that way.

Don and his dog, Nester, walk inside and follow a
hostess to the bar.

"Who are you—?" Caleb looks over his shoulder,
following Rachel's gaze. "Don's here."

"I see," Rachel says, picking up her glass and taking
a sip.

"We should invite him over here," Caleb says.

"No," Rachel says. "We don't have to do that."

"Why not?" Caleb stands up. "I'll go get him."

Rachel lowers her head and covers her face with her
hand.

It's quite unexpected to see Rachel flustered.

She still likes him. They used to date and she still
likes him.

He comes right back, Don and Nester in tow.

"You can sit right here next to Rachel," Caleb says,
reclaiming his seat next to me.

"Hey Rach." Don, wearing his dark sunglasses, sits
down next to her. Nester sits at his feet. "How are you?"

"I'm good." She takes the hands he holds out.

"It's good to see you," Don says, lacing his fingers with
hers.

"You too." Rachel's cheeks are flushed prettily.

The server comes back. Puts a beer in front of Don.

"Here's your beer, Don," she says.

"Bring everyone at the table a beer, will you Abigail?"

"Sure thing." Abigail smiles and turns on her heels, not waiting for a confirmation.

"So," Don says to no one in particular, letting go of Rachel's hands. "Tell me something I don't know."

FORTY-SIX

CALEB

SITTING at the booth with McKenna and Rachel and Don, feels natural.

Abigail brings us all cold bottles of beer.

McKenna takes a sip, frowns, then forces a smile.

"Not really a beer drinker?" I ask, leaning close to her.

"Never developed a taste," she whispers back.

"I find it's best if it's really, really cold," Don says, looking in our direction through his dark sun glasses. "A little frozen on the top. Sort of like a slushy."

"I'll try that," McKenna says, with a glance in my direction.

"Caleb says you're teaching mostly online," Rachel says to Don.

"Yeah. The drive into Glenwood Springs got a little tiresome."

"The drive, huh?" I ask.

"It's hard to find good drivers these days," Don says. "They're always wanting to look at their phones, even when they're driving."

"Isn't that illegal?" I ask.

"Very," McKenna says. "If they get caught."

"Well," Don says. "They don't get caught until something happens."

"That's how it is with everything," McKenna says.

"Right," Don says, looking in Rachel's direction again. "How are things at the store?"

"Steady," Rachel says.

"You ever hire any help?"

"No. You know how I am. I like to do things my way. Come by tomorrow. I'll show you around."

"Oh," Don says. "I would. But I've got a bunch of papers to grade online."

"Bring your computer and hang out," Rachel says. "I've got Internet and I could use the company." She looks at me as though that's suddenly my fault. Not to mention that she's the one who never wanted to hire any help.

"I might just do that," Don says, picking up a menu he can't read. "Do they still have Hawaiian pizza here?"

"I don't know," Rachel says, looking over his shoulder. "Let's take a look."

I look over at McKenna and grin. She smiles back.

It's rather clear that Don has a heightened sense of hearing, so she and I can't have a private conversation with him around.

I'd forgotten that about Don.

It doesn't bother me. It's just something I have to remember when he's around.

"You want cheese, right?" I ask McKenna.

"Yes" she says. "But I'm willing to try something different."

"You can try whatever you want, but you like cheese, so we're getting cheese."

I catch her looking over her shoulder. I know what she's doing. I know she's looking for Silas Crowe.

She'll probably always look for him on some level.

Something like that becomes part of a person's DNA. There's no way to get past it. Not really.

Abigail comes back and we place our order.

"I thought you'd be at the baseball game," Don says.

"We're thinking we'll go by after we eat," I say.

"That's what I always do," Don says.

I catch Rachel's gaze. And I know. Everything suddenly falls into place. She knew that Don would be here. And she timed it just right to be here at the same time he was here.

My sister scares me sometimes.

She sends me a challenging look, daring me to say anything.

I shake my head. Not my business to tell.

Abigail returns to take our order.

"Do you still like pepperoni?" Don asks Rachel.

"You remembered."

"Of course, I did," Don says. Even behind the dark glasses I can see the tenderness in his expression.

McKenna smiles over at me. I put an arm around her and pull her close against me.

This is right.

Everything about tonight is right.

FORTY-SEVEN

McKenna

After we finish our pizza, we all put on our coats and head out to the small-town baseball field, glowing under the floodlights pushing back against the mountain dusk.

The wind is crisp now that the sun is down and I snuggle deeper into the new coat I'm thankful I have. The cool air chills my skin, but Caleb's hand brushes mine, sending little sparks up my arm beneath the chill.

The night air hums with energy as we near the school. Crickets chirp beneath the murmur of conversations and people yell from the bleachers at the crack of a fastball as it slams into a bat. The sounds carry as we near the field.

The scent of popcorn drifting on the breeze mingles

with grilled burgers, a trace of pine needles, and a hint of dust from the field.

Not going inside, we lean against the chain link fence to watch. Lights gleam off helmets, some red, some blue, of high school players. Moths dance in the bright lights and the scoreboard shines with amber numbers.

"Which team is ours?" I ask.

"We're in red," Caleb says.

Something happens out on the field and the crowd cheers in unison.

Caleb takes my hand. "We're winning," he says.

"That's good."

Don and Rachel are standing off to our left. I lean close and whisper in Caleb's ear. "They still like each other."

"They do, don't they?"

"It's sweet. Why did they break up?"

"Like she said, they were young. Then he went blind. I don't know what happened. I don't know if it was an accident or an illness. But he went away for a time. To school. And they just never reconnected."

"Until now." I look past Caleb at Rachel and Don standing close together. "It's good to see Rachel happy."

He follows my gaze. "It's been a long time."

I glance around the little town. So full of innocence.

"I see why you like it here so much," I say. "Everything seems so innocent and wholesome. It's almost like being in a different time. In the past."

"That can be good or bad," he says. "Depending on how you look at it."

"True. There are some things I wouldn't want to give up. Like medical advances."

"We have a doctor here."

"Yes. I'm sure. But Houston is known for its advances in medicine."

"Does this mean you're thinking about staying here permanently?"

Someone hits a homerun and the crowd claps.

"They're clapping for the wrong team," I say.

"Just being polite. Some of the boys on the other team are related."

"Wow. Not what I expected. I thought they were rivals."

"It's complicated. And you changed the subject."

I smile to myself. Yes. Yes. I did change the subject.

"I plead the fifth," I say.

"You're a bit of an enigma," he says.

"Me? No. I'm really just a simple girl at heart."

He pulls me close against him. "Then you'll fit in here just fine."

I give him a lopsided grin. "Presumptuous much?"

"I like to think of myself as persuasive."

Either way he is doing a number on my heart.

And deep down inside, if I look really deep, I know.

He's making me want to stay here.

In this innocent little town that feels like a blast from the past.

"I know what Rachel said." I look up at him, tucking back a strand of hair blown into my face by the wind. "But are you okay if I just sleep in the guest room next to yours?"

"Of course." He glances over toward Rachel and lowers his voice even more. "We just won't tell her."

"Deal."

FORTY-EIGHT

Caleb

"Okay," I say coming out the stock room, my sleeves rolled up. Rachel is sitting on the stool behind the checkout counter. "I got everything unpacked—" I narrow my eyes at her. "What's different about you?"

"What? Nothing," she says.

I glance around the store. "Why are you out here? We're not even open yet."

She stands up and straightens a display of local postcards on a circular rack. "I'm just straightening things up a bit."

"Okay. Well. I've got a flight in a little bit. Will you be okay here by yourself?"

"Of course." She reaches below the counter and holds up her handgun. "I'm ready."

"I guess you are. Be careful with that thing."

"You know I'm well trained."

"Yes." We took the handgun classes together. She's actually a better shot than I am. "But be careful anyway. You don't want to be taken by surprise."

"I'll be careful."

"Is that why you're sitting out here? To keep watch?"

"No," she says primly. "I'm waiting for someone."

"Someone." I narrow my eyes. "Don? Is Don coming by?"

"Yes. He's got someone who can drop him off on their way into Boulder so he's going to work in my office for awhile. Then we're going to go to lunch."

I grin. "It's like a day date."

"You're weird."

"Already established. But I feel better having someone with you while I'm not here." I tilt my head to the side. "You do know that Don is blind, right?"

"I noticed. And you're saying that why?"

"Because you curled your hair."

"I always curl my hair."

I shake my head. "Maybe. But you left it down."

"How did things go with McKenna last night?" She promptly changes the subject.

"She slept in the guest room."

"I thought we said she'd sleep in your room."

"You said."

"Whatever." She shrugs. "Where's your flight to?"

"Just Denver. Want coffee before I go?"

"You know I do."

A car pulls up at the door and stops. "That must be Don."

"He's early," she says, running her hands nervously down her skirt.

"I'll let him in."

I unlock the door and let Don and Nester inside. "Good morning, Don. Come on in here."

"How's it going Caleb?"

"Good. I'm heading down to the coffee shop. You want anything?"

"Sure. Do they have those cold brews?"

"I'm guessing they do."

"Good." He pulls a credit card out of his pocket. "Get everyone something on me."

"Not happening. You bought dinner last night."

He presses the credit card into my hand. "I insist."

I take it and drop it into my pocket, but I won't use it. What is it with people suddenly wanting to pay for everything?

I glance at my watch.

I have just enough time to get everyone coffee, get back here with it, and get to the airfield.

FORTY-NINE

McKenna

I wake the next morning feeling more rested than I have in a long time.

Much better than sleeping in strange hotel rooms. Even better than I'd slept when I'd stayed with Miles and Tabby. Of course, that was right after Jennie, so I wouldn't have slept well anywhere at that particular time.

But there's something about sleeping in the room next to Caleb with Rachel in her room down the hallway that had me feeling safe and sleeping soundly.

I don't think I would have slept soundly if I'd slept in Caleb's room, not even with him on the sofa, but for different reasons.

I turn on the water in the shower and gather up clean clothes to put on while the water heats up.

The house is obviously older, but it's been renovated. The bathroom is spacious with both a large shower and a free-standing bathtub which I might have to try out sooner rather than later.

Standing in the shower, I let the hot water run over my head until it starts to cool. Not a very considerate guest, I suppose, but the hot water is irresistible.

I put on a pair of jeans and layer a cardigan over a long-sleeve cotton shirt. It's past time for me to do laundry, considering that most of my clothes are business clothes. And yet since I rarely wear them, I hadn't realized just how many casual clothes I had.

I'm mostly finished drying my hair when someone knocks on my door.

My heart lodges in my throat even though I know that Silas Crowe would not come to the door and knock. I'm just jumpy. It's obviously either Rachel or Caleb.

Still barefoot, I walk to the door and open it.

Caleb is standing there holding a large paper cup from the coffee shop.

"Hi," he says. "I thought you might want coffee."

"Yes," I say, taking the cup. "But I could have gotten it."

"I know, but I had to go anyway and I'm heading out for a flight to Denver."

"Oh." That's disappointing. "Thank you. It was very thoughtful."

"Do you need anything else before I head to the airfield?"

"I don't think so." I shift from one bare foot to the other.

He glances at my bare feet. "Do we need to make another trip to Mrs. Chan's?"

"No. I have boots. Well. Maybe."

He grins. "We'll go when I get back. See if she has some trail boots."

"Trail boots." I smile back. "I've never had trail boots."

"A necessity around here."

My smile falters as I remember why I'm here.

"Are you sure you're going to be okay?" he asks, tucking a strand of still slightly damp hair off my face.

"I'll be okay. I'll go help Rachel in the store."

"About that."

"What? Am I in trouble again?"

"No. But she has a guest."

"Don?"

"Yes. He's hanging out and they're going to lunch."

"I guess I'm on my own then."

"Just for a little while. I'll be back. Don't make any plans for dinner."

"What kind of plans would I make?"

"I don't know. I'm sure by the time I get back you'll have men lined up at the door to take you out."

I laugh. "Right. Not likely."

"Not to be overprotective," he says. "But don't go far, okay?"

"I won't. I think I'll sit in front of the fireplace and read a good novel."

"Sounds like the perfect way to spend the day."

"It sounds decadent to me, but I'm going to try it anyway." I literally cannot remember the last time I had a day to spend doing nothing but reading.

I take a sip of the hot coffee. Caleb seems reluctant to leave.

"I'll be okay."

He leans forward and kisses me on the cheek. "See you soon."

I smile and close the door after he walks away.

I'm breaking so many of my own rules.

But I can't help it. Caleb is handsome and charming and he gives me butterflies in my stomach.

What's a girl to do?

CHAPTER
FIFTY

RACHEL

"Are you okay back here? Do you need anything?"

I stand at the door to my office and look at Don sitting in my chair, his laptop computer opened up in front of him.

"I've got everything I need." He looks back at me with unseeing eyes.

"What about the security monitors? Will they bother you? Do you want me to turn them off?"

"If you turn them off, how can I know you're there?"

I look at him sideways. I don't know how to answer that. Don is legally blind. How will having the monitors on help him know if I'm okay?

In that uncanny way of his, he seems to read my mind. "You can turn the volume up."

"Really? You want the volume up?"

"I wouldn't mind. It lets me know I'm not here by myself."

"Okay." I get that. I really do. I turn up the volume enough that he can hear what's going on out in the store. "How's that?"

"I don't hear anything."

"There's nothing to hear, Silly. The volume in right here." I take his hand and guide him to the volume button.

"Got it," he says.

"Just adjust it however you want."

The little bell over the front door rings.

"Sounds like you have a customer," he says.

"Okay. I'll see you later."

I turn around and head out into the store.

A bearded man wearing a heavy coat stands just inside the door. His hands in his pockets. He is surveying the store as though taking stock.

"Welcome to the Outpost," I say. "Are you looking for anything in particular?"

At first I don't think he's going to answer. Then. "No," he says, not looking at me. "I'm just taking a look around."

"Okay. Take your time. Don't hesitate to ask if you need anything."

The man makes a grunting sound that I take as agreement.

He walks over to the hiking supplies and stands there, his hands still in his pockets, but I get the sense that he's not really looking at anything.

I don't really care. Maybe he's just killing time while his wife does some shopping. Happens all the time.

I go behind the counter and straighten up some tour guides we keep near the register.

After a few minutes, the man wanders up to the counter and stands there.

"Can I help you with something?" I ask with a little smile. I think I liked it better when he didn't look at me.

The man just looks in my direction a moment. "Where do people stay? When they're just passing through?"

"Are you looking for a place to stay?" I ask.

He doesn't say anything.

"There are a few rooms here and there, but most people stay at the Alpine Falls Lodge. It's just outside of town."

"What about a hotel?"

"We don't have any hotels in Alpine Falls. If you don't want to stay at the lodge, you can drive into Boulder. There are plenty of hotels there."

He doesn't say anything. He just looks at me with bottomless black eyes.

I go back to straightening the brochures, but honestly, there's something creepy about him.

It takes all kinds, I guess.

"What about those rooms?" he asks. "How do I find them?"

"You have to ask the shop owners," I say, suddenly wanting to get rid of him. "They would be the ones to know what's available."

"What about you?" he asks, pinning me with those eyes. "Do you have a room?"

"I—"

"Rachel," Don comes out of the back, stopping just at the door. "Can you help me with something?"

"Of course. I just—"

"It's urgent."

"Excuse me," I say to the customer. "I'll be right back."

I leave him, following Don back to the office.

"You didn't bring Nester," I say. "Or your cane. Are you okay?" And he's not wearing his dark glasses.

Using his hands, he finds his way back around the desk. "Look," he says.

I follow and look at the monitors.

The bell over the door rings as the man steps outside.

"He left," I say.

Don sits down and I sit on the desk in front of him.

"You needed to get away from that man," Don says.

"Why? He was asking for a place to stay."

"No. He wasn't. He was up to something."

"I don't know..."

"Rach. I want you to stay away from that man. If he comes back here. If you see him on the street. Stay away from him."

"Okay."

"There's something evil about him."

"How do you know that?"

"Haven't you heard that blind people have heightened senses?"

"Of course."

"Well. I have a heightened sense about him. When Caleb gets back, show him the recording. Humor me."

"Okay. I'll show him."

A little chill runs along my spine.

I don't know what Don sensed about the customer, but I'm glad the man is out of my shop. And I hope he doesn't come back.

FIFTY-ONE

CALEB

I MAKE it into Denver just fine, but there's a weather delay getting out.

My clients are a young couple on their honeymoon, so they don't care one way or another. They're just happy no matter what. Whispering to each other and snuggling together.

I, on the other hand, am ready to get back to Alpine Falls.

Now that I know that someone is after McKenna, I don't like leaving her alone.

I guess I come by that particular trait honestly. My

mother refuses to leave our father. She gave up everything to be with him.

Standing at the window looking out over the tarmac with the grounded planes, watching the lightning light up the bruised sky, I wonder if this means I've found my one true love.

McKenna.

I don't discount the way I'm feeling. I was besotted by her the moment I first saw her standing at the depot.

Love at first sight perhaps. They say that's how it happens. Like a bolt of lightning.

Watching the couple in the reflection of the window, I feel like maybe that's exactly what happened.

I was hit by a bolt of lightning.

Cupid's arrow.

Whatever one chooses to call it, I have to accept that I've fallen head over heels with McKenna.

Just being around her makes me come alive. When I'm away from her, she's all I can think about.

It sounds like it would be a simple boy meets girl fairy tale story, but it's not that simple.

She has a killer after her for one thing.

Because of that, she's not safe anywhere. I'd had to make her promise she wouldn't run from Alpine Falls after she thought she saw the man who did it. Silas Crowe.

If something happens to her while she's in Alpine Falls, I'll never forgive myself.

My job is to keep her safe no matter what.

And, dammit.

If keeping her safe means letting her go, then that's what I'll have to do.

Surely there's another way.

A better way than letting her go.

She can't just live her life running.

When I get back, I've got to get her to the sheriff. I should have already done that, but she seemed like she needed a break from thinking all that.

Maybe Sheriff Bradley Winslow will have some insight on some other options.

Even if she doesn't want to tell me where she's from and where the murder of her friend happened, maybe she'll tell him.

Maybe she'll tell him so he can help her.

We've got to figure out a way to keep her from having to run.

It's possible she'll want to go back to wherever she's from. That's okay. I can deal with that. At least if I know where that is.

What I can't deal with is her out there running from place to place. Fearing for her life.

That's what I've got to help her do something about.

And maybe, just maybe, she'll make the choice to stay in Alpine Falls.

It's a stretch. Not too many people do.

But it's a possibility. And as long as it's a possibility, I have hope.

CHAPTER

FIFTY-TWO

McKenna

I FINISHED READING the novel I'd already started and picked out another one to read next.

I didn't, however, start the new one. I needed to give myself time to process the one I finished first. It had a satisfying end, but one I didn't expect.

Getting up and walking around, I realize I'd skipped lunch. Just like old times. As an attorney, I often skipped lunch, whether because I was in court or because I was buried in court case review or trial preparation.

It hadn't taken me long to get into the habit of eating regular meals.

Eight days, a glance at the calendar Rachel has in the

kitchen tells me. Eight days since the day Jennie had been killed.

The reality of it still catches me off guard at odd times.

I'll do something or even think about something and think about how I should tell Jennie when I talk to her next time.

It's devastating when reality sweeps over me that I won't be able to ever tell her anything else comes crashing in on the heels of whatever I'd been thinking about telling her.

So for about a week I've been eating three meals a days. Not particularly out of hunger, but because it demarcates the day.

My stomach, though, doesn't understand why I suddenly skipped a meal.

Since I'd promised Caleb I wouldn't go far, I don't leave the house. Walking the streets of Alpine Falls by myself right now doesn't feel like something I'm ready to do. I'm too ensconced in a feeling of safety right here right now to leave.

So I find a rice cake in the pantry and call it lunch. Then I lay down on the sofa in front of the fireplace and take a nap.

I wake with a jolt when I hear someone coming in the back door.

I sit up straight hold the throw blanket over me like a shield. For good measure I grab a little decorative pillow and hold it in my lap.

Then I forget to take a breath.

When Caleb comes in through the back door, I take a gulp of air and put a hand over my chest. "You scared me half to death," I say.

"I'm sorry. You've got plenty of protection there."

"Protection?"

"The pillow and the blanket."

"Oh." I set the pillow aside. "I fell asleep."

"In that case," he says, sitting down next to me. "I'm sorry I woke you."

"It's okay. I don't normally nap. Not that I mind. It's just I never had time."

"Really? Not even on the weekends."

"Weekends are for errands and catching up on work that didn't get done during the week."

"I think maybe you work too much."

"Did. Did work too much anyway. Not working at the moment."

"I'm sure Alpine Falls can use a good psychologist. We don't have one, you know."

"I'll keep that in mind," I say, pulling my bare feet back up under me, not even bothering to explain that I'm not a psychologist. "How was your flight?"

"Weather delayed," he says. "I got back as soon as I could."

"You didn't have to hurry."

"Did anything happen while I was gone?"

"I don't—"

"Yes," Rachel says coming into the living room with Don and Nester in tow.

I hadn't heard her come inside. Unlike Caleb, Rachel come into the house without a sound.

Caleb looks questioningly at me. I shrug. "I've been here all day."

Rachel sits in the armchair and Don sits on the arm of it next to her. Nester drops into a sitting position next to him.

"At ease, Nester," Don says. Nester lies down, putting one front paw over his face for an impromptu nap.

"What happened?" Caleb asks.

Rachel opens up her iPad and mirrors it onto the television screen.

"We need you to look at something," she says. "Someone came into the shop today."

Everything inside me turns inside out.

I don't know what she has there on her iPad, but the possibilities are terrifying.

Sitting on terrifying pins and needles, I watch the footage of the inside of the store starts.

FIFTY-THREE

CALEB

WE SIT in silence as Rachel pulls up the footage she's looking for.

"Don is the one who realized something wasn't right. I didn't notice it until I played back the footage."

"You couldn't see it because you were in it," Don says, taking her hand.

"It might not be anything," Rachel says.

I glance over at McKenna. She's pale as a sheet. "Are you okay?" I ask.

She shakes her head. "No," she whispers. "Not really."

The bell over the door to the shop rings through loud and clear on the video. Our cameras are almost too good.

"This is it," Rachel says.

I watch the screen as a bearded man comes in through the door. He's wearing a heavy coat and keeps his hands in his pockets.

At first I don't recognize his face. Not with the beard. But I recognize his size and the way he holds himself.

"That's him," McKenna says, her voice less than a whisper.

"Silas Crowe?" I ask, taking her hand.

She nods.

I feel her trembling as she sits through the video. She watches as Don comes to the door. No cane. No dog. No glasses. Just a guy coming to the door asking for, no demanding, help. Thank heavens Don was there.

And very smart on his part. He's showed no vulnerability whatsoever.

When the bell over the door rings again and Silas steps out of the shop, McKenna gets up without a word and dashes up the stairs.

I let her go. I'll go to her in a few minutes. But first, there's something Don needs to know about. He's inadvertently part of it now and he deserves to know what's going on. Rachel may have already told him, but I tell him anyway.

With Rachel sitting quietly, I tell Don what we know.

"You've got to get her to the sheriff," Don says, holding Rachel's hands in both of his. "It's not safe for her here. He's looking for McKenna. And it's not safe for Rachel either.

"You're right. We'll go tomorrow."

Don leans toward Rachel. "I don't think you should be alone in the shop until this guy is arrested."

"I'll be okay. I know what he looks like now."

"Rach," he says. "I don't want to lose you. Not after being apart from you all these years."

"I'm going up to check on McKenna," I say. This is one of those times to give Rachel and Don privacy.

Stopping at the guest room, I knock on the door. "McKenna?"

No answer.

"McKenna? Are you okay?"

When she doesn't answer, I try the doorknob. It isn't locked. I crack it open. "McKenna?"

Dammit. I push the door open and step inside. Her two suitcases are open the bed. She's walking from the closet, her arms full of clothes.

"McKenna. Wait."

She throws the clothes on the bed, but doesn't look at me. With hands trembling, she starts folding.

Going on instinct, I wrap my arms around her. She's trembling, but otherwise goes still.

Pressing her head against my chest, I hold her tight.

She takes a deep breath. Lets it out slowly.

"I can't do it," she whispers. "I can't stay here and put Rachel in danger.

"Leaving won't help," I say. "He already knows you're here."

She stills. "Oh God."

"It's okay. He can't hurt you. He can't hurt Rachel. You're safe here."

"That's what I thought." She presses her fingers into my back, holding on. "Jennie. Jennie was safe. In my condo. There was a valet. A concierge. He didn't have a key fob for the elevator. He got inside the condo anyway."

I hold her tight. Feeling the fear coursing through her. "How?" I ask.

"I don't know."

Relaxing my hold on her, I pull out my cell phone.

Send a quick text.

This has gone on too long for me to not do anything.

"Leaving here won't fix it," I say. "If you leave, he could follow you." And it still wouldn't protect Rachel. Rachel could end up just like Jennie. Collateral damage or revenge or whatever justification a sick mind like Silas Crowe comes up with.

She takes a ragged breath. "He was here. He talked to Rachel."

"And Don was here with her. Neither one of you will be left alone."

"But you," she says, looking into my eyes. "What about you?"

"I'll be okay. I was in Special Forces, remember?"

"Right. But still. He's dangerous. In an underhanded kind of way."

"We're going to put a stop to this," I say.

The doorbell rings, echoing through the house.

McKenna jolts, startled.

"It's Sheriff Bradley Winslow."

"You called the sheriff?"

"Texted. He and I go way back. He's a good guy."

"The Houston cops didn't find him," she says.

"Maybe they didn't have a personal stake in this like we do. It's one of the many perks of living in a small town."

"What do I tell him?"

"You tell him everything. If you don't tell him everything, he can't help us."

"Okay," she says with ragged breath. "I'll tell him everything."

"That's my girl. You ready?"

"No," she says with a little half smile. "Not really."

"Let's get it over with. Then we'll make something for dinner. Do you like spaghetti?"

"Who doesn't?" She looks at me sideways. "You cook?"

"I make the best spaghetti in town."

"Okay. Let's do it."

FIFTY-FOUR

McKENNA

SHERIFF BRADLEY WINSLOW is a kind and perceptive man.

He seems to know just what to ask and yet he doesn't push me too much. Maybe it helps that Caleb sits next to me on the sofa, holding my hand.

Rachel and Don vanished into the kitchen. Hearing them in there, having normal conversations... doing normal things... is comforting, too.

Bradley watched the video. Sends it to himself.

"I'd like to contact the authorities where this happened," Bradley says. "It would be helpful if I could work with them."

I glance at Caleb then back to the sheriff. "I understand

that. I haven't told Caleb where it happened. I don't want to put him and Rachel at risk. The less they know... right?"

"That's admirable," Bradley says. "But Silas Crowe has obviously found you. I think all you're doing now is protecting him and I don't think that's your intent."

"No," I say, letting out a breath. "That's anything but my intent. Can I borrow some paper? Your pen?"

"Sure." He hands his little spiral notebook, turned to a fresh page, and his pen over to me.

I write down the case number. The phone number of the detective. Two things I memorized the minute I had them. "This will get you to someone who knows everything."

"I knew you were from the south," Caleb says, seeing the phone number.

"Didn't say you were wrong," I say, squeezing his hand.

"Let me call and get to work on this," Bradley tells me. Then looks to Caleb. "This man is obviously dangerous. Don't leave her or your sister alone."

"Don't worry. We won't. I'll walk you out."

I sit on the sofa, staring into the flames as Caleb walks the sheriff out.

I don't know if Caleb can keep me safe from Silas.

But if anyone can, he can.

I do know that I stand a much better chance of staying safe here with Caleb than I would out there by myself.

He's right about that.

So there's that.

There's also a new part about me not wanting to leave Caleb. I've gotten rather attached to him.

Rachel and Don's laughter drifts from the kitchen, warming my heart.

Even with the devastation that got me here, I somehow landed in a place unlike any I've known before. A place where I feel at peace.

Caleb is the biggest part of that. I can admit that. It's Caleb that anchors me here.

Maybe Alpine Falls is a place I could call home. Maybe. One day.

FIFTY-FIVE

Caleb

Normalcy.

Something to strive for and hard to maintain considering everything that's happening.

Don and Rachel, after putting homemade bread in the bread maker, are in the living room, looking for a movie to watch later. Rachel reads the descriptions to him and adds her own commentary about the pictures on the screen.

While I mix the tomato sauce for the spaghetti, McKenna chops veggies. So far I haven't found anything she can't do and do well.

I reduce the heat on the tomato sauce and check to see how she's coming.

Tears are streaming down her cheeks.

"McKenna," I say, hurrying to her. "What's wrong?"

"Onions," she says, looking at me with red eyes.

"Oh sweetness. Why didn't you say something?"

"I thought I could get through it."

"Come here." Pulling her toward the freezer, I open the door and guide her to stand in front of it. "There may be a better solution, but this always works for me."

She wipes at her face and leans forward into the cold air.

"This is helping," she says.

I get her a cool wet cloth and place it gently over her eyes.

"I'll be okay." She steps back and does look like she's in less agony.

"You sit down. I'll finish the chopping."

"I won't argue." She sits on one of the bar stools at the island, pressing the cool cloth against her eyes.

"You're almost finished with these onions. Let me get them out of here."

"This doesn't usually happen to me," she says.

"You cook a lot?"

"No. I guess that could be why it doesn't usually happen."

I slide the chopped onions into the tomato sauce. "You're a funny girl."

She smiles. "I don't get accused of that very often."

"I would think psychologists have to be serious."

"I would think so, too. But... as much as I admire the field of psychology and even though I do have a minor in psychology, it's not my field."

"A minor. So I was close."

She smiles and straightens on the stool. "Yes. I guess you were close."

I add the chopped green peppers to my growing mixture before sitting down next to her. "Maybe you'll tell me one day what it is you did in Houston."

"Since you know pretty much everything now," she says. "I guess there's not much point in you not knowing."

"I'm not seeing one."

"Are you sure you want to know?"

I consider that a moment. Run through a few things through my head that I haven't considered before. "I promise whatever it is, I won't judge."

"Okay then," she says, looking at me with her teal green eyes. "You had every chance to back out of knowing." She pauses. "I'm an attorney."

"An attorney. I wasn't too far off."

"How do you figure that?"

I get up to stir my sauce. "An attorney." I look at her over my shoulder. "Like a psychologist. Has to understand people."

"That's a good point."

"It's a very good point. Wine?"

"Sure."

I select a bottle of red wine from the wine rack and open it. Pour some into two glasses, handing one to her.

"So," I say, sitting next to her again. "What kind of attorney?"

She swirls her wine. Takes a sip. "This is good. Prosecuting."

"Ah. I see. I have a feeling this has something to do with Silas Crowe."

"You would be right."

"You failed to mention that to the sheriff."

"Did I? It didn't seem relevant."

I narrow my eyes at her. "You know everything is relevant."

"He'll get that information from the detective."

"Fair enough." But I still think she should have told him. I'm not an attorney, but it seems relevant to me.

If Silas Crowe is after revenge, it's a much more powerful motive than it seemed at first.

She takes another sip of her wine. "I think you're right. It is relevant."

I nod.

"Do you have your phone? We should call the sheriff."

"No. We should let Sheriff Winslow do his job. And we just enjoy our evening. We're going to have my famous homemade spaghetti. And we're going to watch a movie."

She leans close. "Can Don watch a movie?"

"You'd be surprised what Don gets from dialogue. And Rachel will be his eyes when needed."

"It's like they've been a couple forever."

"They're cute together, aren't they?"

"They are."

"Okay," Rachel comes into the kitchen, Don behind her. "We need less talking and more cooking."

"There's plenty of cooking going on in here," I say. "But I'm glad you're here to check on your bread before I have to do it."

"He knows not to touch the bread machine," Rachel says.

"We found a movie," Don says. "I think you'll like it."

"What kind of movie is it?" McKenna asks.

"It's a romance," Don says.

No one says anything for a moment.

"Wait," I say. "Rachel picked out a romance movie?"

Don looks a bit sheepish. "I might've had something to do with picking out the movie."

"Don had more than a little bit to do with it," Rachel says as she lifts the bread out of the machine.

"I'm just in shock that she agreed to it," I say. "Don. You're a good influence on my sister."

"She's not so bad," Don says, leaning against the counter.

"When you boys finish talking about me, one of you can take a knife and start slicing this bread."

"I'm think that would be me," I say, taking the bread knife from the drawer and getting to work.

"I'll stir the sauce," McKenna says.

"Watch out for those onions," I tell her.

"These onions had their chance."

I smile over at my sister.

Tonight is good. One of the best I can remember us ever having.

Rachel and I have worked hard to keep our family business going. Tonight it feels like it's paid off. Tonight it feels like a lot of things have finally paid off.

Rachel has reunited with Don. And I've found McKenna.

All is right with our world.

I couldn't ask for anything more.

FIFTY-SIX

McKenna

After a delicious homemade spaghetti dinner with homemade bread and ice cream for dessert, we watched the romance movie Don picked out.

All four of us sat on the sectional with the fire glowing beneath the television screen. Don and Rachel sat close together holding hands as did Caleb and I. Caleb and I sat snuggled up together, his arm around me.

It was all cozy and normal. And for a little while I almost forgot about the danger of Silas Crowe being out there, possibly even knowing where I am.

He was here. He talked to Rachel. I know it was him. I saw him on the video.

He's wearing a beard now, making it harder to recognize him. But I did. I recognized him. I heard the flat undertone of threat in his voice. Most, like Rachel, took the tone as apathy. But I heard it and I know what it was. Coiled threat.

Don heard it, too. He heard it and he got Rachel out of there. Don is not a small man and the way he came out of the back room, no dark glasses, no cane, no seeing eye dog, he no doubt looked formidable enough for Silas to take his leave. Smart move on Don's part. Very smart.

As the credits play and Rachel turns the lights on, Caleb looks over at Don. "Do you need a ride home?" he asks.

"No. I'm just going to sleep here on the sofa."

"He's going to stay here until this thing," Rachel flicks an apologetic glance in my direction. "Is taken care of. I'll drive him home tomorrow to get some clothes and things."

"Okay," Caleb says. "That's going above and beyond, Don."

"I'm an above and beyond kind of guy," Don says.

"Yes you are. "Caleb stands up and holds out a hand for me. "Ready for me to walk you upstairs?"

Thinking that's his way of suggesting we give Don and Rachel some time alone, I put a hand in his and let him pull me to my feet.

"Good movie," I say. "I liked it. Thanks Rachel and Don."

"I liked it, too," Don says.

"It wasn't bad," Rachel chimes in, sitting down again next to Don and pulling her feet up under her.

"You liked it," Don says, teasingly.

She shrugs. "Maybe."

"Good night," Caleb says.

"Good night," I say as he leads me toward the stairs. "They're so cute," I say to Caleb as we walk upstairs.

"I'm pleased they reconnected."

We reach my door and stop.

"Well," I say. "This is me."

"Funny."

I smile.

He puts one hand on the door frame and the other on my cheek.

"I had a nice time tonight," I say.

"So did I. I'm glad you're here."

"Yeah." My smile flounders with an image of just how I ended up here.

"That won't ever completely go away," he says. "But it helps if you can think about something else."

"I try."

"I can help." He takes a step closer.

"How can you do that?" I lift my chin a little and meet his gaze. I have some ideas about how I think he could help distract me.

Instead though, he looks up toward a sound behind us. Like a box falling to the floor.

"Did you hear something?" I whisper.

"Sounded like rats in the attic."

"I heard it, too."

"We don't have rats."

I swallow thickly and follow his gaze toward the ceiling of my room. "What do you think it was?"

"Probably a bird got in the attic or a chipmunk."

"Oh." Relief floods through me that he has a good explanation.

"Do you need to go up and get it out?"

"They usually get themselves out," he says, but he still looks troubled.

"You don't look convinced," I say.

"Just jumpy. I'm sure it's nothing to worry about."

"Surely," I say.

"Why don't you sleep in my room tonight?" he asks, still looking up towards the ceiling.

I raise an eyebrow.

He grins. "I'll sleep on the sofa."

"Okay." It must be something in his expression that has me wary. Whatever it is, the noise in the attic, his expression, he has me not wanting to spend the night in this room by myself.

"I'll just wait here," he says. "While you get ready for bed."

I don't know what he thinks will happen. That something (someone) will suddenly crash through the ceiling and attack me. But... if he wants to wait, then I'll let him wait.

"I won't be long." I go into the bathroom, close the door,

and proceed to get ready for bed. My hands tremble a bit as I brush out my hair and pull it back to wash my face.

I don't know if I'm nervous because we heard something in the attic or if it's because Silas Crowe is out there and I saw him on the recording or if I'm nervous because I'm going to be sleeping in the same room with Caleb.

As I brush my teeth, I decide it's a little bit of all of the above, but mostly the latter.

I've been through so much in the last few days that a little noise in the attic doesn't concern me all that much. Compared to what I've been through, a chipmunk in the attic is stunningly nothing.

But Caleb. Caleb is a different story altogether. Just knowing that he's waiting for me on the other side of the bathroom door has my system thrumming with nerves.

Yep. It's definitely Caleb that has my nerves on edge.

I smile to myself as I get into my pajamas. The way I feel about Caleb is a good thing. It's been so long since I felt this way that I almost didn't recognize the feeling.

I *like* him. Like REALLY like him.

I'll happily take this feeling over all other possible feelings any day.

FIFTY-SEVEN

Caleb

McKenna steps out of the bathroom wearing her long pajamas. Cute. Reminds me of Rachel when she was a little girl.

Also reminds me of just how innocent McKenna seems.

And I'm in charge of protecting that innocence.

Even if it means protecting her from myself.

I'd been poised to kiss her right before we heard something in the attic.

I'd told McKenna it was probably a bird or a chipmunk. The problem is... well... I lied. Sort of. Nothing can get in the attic. I know because I'm the one who nailed the screens over all the openings.

I'll go up tomorrow and see if one came loose. If it did, I'll get whatever animal found its way inside out of there and repair the screen.

If not, then we may have other problems.

But right now I'm not going to think about that.

Right now I'm going to enjoy how cute McKenna looks in her gray bear-printed pajamas and bare feet.

I'm going to have to get her some slippers before winter. When winter gets here, her feet are going to freeze.

"All set?" I ask.

"Yes. Let me just grab my book." She stops by the night-stand to pick up a paperback. Most people, everyone else, would've had to stop for their cell phone charger.

"You know. We can get you a cell phone. With a new number."

"Good idea. I can change it to my old number later."

Or not. It would be okay with me if she let go of her old life as an attorney in Houston.

But. Being an attorney in Houston isn't the kind of thing anyone would let go of. She worked too hard for it and unlike me, she doesn't have a family business keeping her from the city.

I have to back off of the plans I had on kissing her. First of all, I can't be kissing her when I'm charged with protecting her innocence. And second, I don't need to kiss her when I know good and well she'll be going back to Houston as soon as Silas Crowe is back behind bars again.

Things I didn't think of in the moment before we were interrupted.

She never said anything differently about going back to Houston and I have to respect that.

"We'll go into town, tomorrow," I say as I turn back the bed linens for her. "Get you a phone. I need to at least be able to text you. Right?"

"Right." She sits down on the edge of the bed. "Is that couch going to be comfortable you think?"

"I think it'll be just fine. That's one thing about being in the military. You learn to sleep anywhere."

"Okay. I'll try not to feel bad about taking the bed."

"Don't. I'm going to get us some water and some blankets for the couch while you get settled in."

"Okay. Thanks."

And I'm also going to remind Rachel to lock her bedroom door tonight.

I won't tell her I heard something over McKenna's room. She'll have me calling the sheriff. Either that or going up there to look around myself. I'll go up there in the morning, but not going tonight. Locking her door and having Don with his keen ears downstairs should take care of any potential problems.

I also need to take a minute to get my mind off of kissing McKenna.

FIFTY-EIGHT

McKenna

I READ JUST over a page in my book before I'm yawning.

One way for me to make things easier is to be asleep when Caleb gets back.

He was going to kiss me. Had been a breath away from kissing me when we heard something in the attic over the guest room.

A girl knows when a man is about to kiss her and Caleb had been so close to kissing me.

Probably not the best idea to let him kiss me.

So I set my book aside and turn off the lamp, letting darkness slide into the room. No street lights out here to break the darkness behind the shades.

I settle in beneath the sheets that smell like Caleb and pretend to sleep.

He's gone longer than I expected and I almost did actually drift off to sleep, but I wake up when he sets a water bottle on the nightstand.

"Everything okay?" I ask, forgetting that I was supposed to be sleeping.

"I thought you were asleep."

"I was." Sort of.

"I was just reminding Rachel to lock her door."

"You didn't tell her about the chipmunk?" I can't see him in the darkness, but I can tell by his voice that he's not standing far away.

"No. She'd have me going up there in the dark."

I smile to myself, knowing he's right.

"Rachel is an interesting woman."

"You can say that again."

"What do you think about Don staying over?"

Caleb's at the sofa now, tossing a blanket over it. I don't know he can see in the complete darkness.

"Don's a good guy. I appreciate him watching out for Rachel."

"Do you think they'll get together?"

I hear him sit on the sofa and take off one boot, then the other, dropping them one by one onto the floor. "We can hope."

I open my bottle of water and take a sip. "Did Rachel ever date anyone else?"

"Nothing serious. I think she always liked Don."

"That's sweet."

He stretched out on the couch and I imagine him putting his hands behind his head. "You want to go up in the helicopter tomorrow?"

"Really?" I ask, forgetting to sound sleepy.

"Maybe. We should probably see what the sheriff finds out."

"He won't find out much."

"Why do you say that?"

"There are procedures required for him to get that kind of information."

"Right. I guess it's not so simple as picking up the phone anymore."

"Not so much. I'm not sure if that's a good thing or a bad thing."

"It's just a thing, I guess." He sounds sleepy. I rather like his sleepy voice. I like everything about him.

"You locked the door?" I ask.

"Yes. I did. Are you worried?"

"How could I be worried? With Don keeping watch downstairs and you right there. Nah. I'm not worried."

But deep down, I guess I am a little bit worried.

Silas Crowe got past all sorts of people he shouldn't have gotten past and he killed Jennie. Then he got right back out past those same people.

I still don't know how he did it. That he was able to do that terrifies me. Someone who has that kind of skill would have no problem getting inside this house unseen. Killing all us. Then leaving just as unseen as he had been getting in to start with.

But I don't tell Caleb all that. Those are my thoughts and fears and I'll keep them to myself. Some thoughts are better kept to oneself.

Most especially when the person I would tell is the very same person I'd like very much to kiss.

"Good night, sweetness," Caleb says from across the room.

"Good night."

How is it Caleb knows exactly how to distract me from my own worrisome thoughts?

Somehow he does. And somehow it works.

Now I'm thinking about him again.

It's a good system.

CHAPTER

FIFTY-NINE

CALEB

THE NEXT MORNING we wake to a thunderstorm.

My first thought is the same thought that I always have when it rains. I won't be flying today. Or at least not this morning. I instinctively grab my phone and check the weather.

Nope. Not flying today.

That's unfortunate. I'd been hoping to take McKenna up today. Mostly to distract her from the news that Silas Crowe has come to town.

It's okay. We'll go another day. I'll find another way to distract her.

It can't be random that Silas Crowe is here. It's not possible that it's random. The country is too big and Alpine Falls is too far away from Houston for him to just randomly show up here. In the Outpost. He found a way to track her.

Maybe it's important to know just when she ditched her car and her phone. Maybe he planted some kind of tracker in her luggage.

That would be a bold move on his part. Very bold and very wily.

It would take access to technology and some serious skills. But it could happen. Especially so since Silas had been in prison. Prison, from what I understand, is a training ground for criminals. They go in knowing a little and come out experts. Apparently he escaped so he has skills.

But right now I don't want to wake McKenna so I go quietly into the bathroom, shower, shave, and get dressed.

Then I slip out of the bedroom and head downstairs to make coffee.

Don and Rachel are already up, sitting at the breakfast table eating what looks like breakfast burritos.

"Good morning," I say. "You two are up early."

"I'm always up early," Rachel says, sending me a vexed glance.

"I'm a light sleeper," Don says.

"Did you hear anything in the night?" I ask him, pausing with a hand halfway to the cabinet door.

"Nothing," he says.

"Huh. I've got to go up into the attic. See if one of the screens maybe came loose."

"Why?" Rachel asks, pinning me with a gaze. She knows I would not go into the attic without a good reason.

I take a mug from the cabinet and switch on the coffee machine.

I turn and face her. She's going to be mad I didn't tell her last night. "Heard something," I murmur.

"What did you hear?"

"I don't know, Rachel. That's—"

"Caleb!" McKenna yells from the second floor. I hear the alarm in her voice.

I shoot away from the cabinet, around the island, and dash up the stairs. I find her standing in the middle of the guest room facing the direction of the bathroom.

"What's wrong?"

She holds up an arm, pointing toward the bathroom. I follow her gaze.

Rachel and Don come up silently behind me.

Words written in red are scrawled on the bathroom mirror. I take a step forward so I can see better.

You're next.

"What the—?" I glance over at McKenna. She's white as a sheet. Not moving.

Leaning forward, I sniff the red on the mirror. "Lipstick." I turn back to McKenna. "Is this your lipstick?" I ask. I've never seen her wear red lipstick. Not this bright red color.

"Jennie," she chokes out.

"Jennie?"

"Jennie's lipstick."

With one more glance at the bright red lipstick shade, I walk over to McKenna and pull her into my arms.

Rachel has her phone out. "I'm calling Bradley."

"It's okay," I say to McKenna. "I'm here. We're here."

"How did he get in here?" McKenna asks, her voice muffled against my shoulder. I don't think she's looking for an answer. I think she's just wondering out loud.

Don, using his cane, walks the perimeter of the room.

"So many ways," he says, also talking to himself. "The window. The door, of course." He stops and looks up toward the ceiling. "You said you heard something up there."

"We did."

Rachel comes up to stand next to him.

"What are you thinking, Don?" she asks.

"Describe to me what you see."

"Let's go downstairs to wait for the sheriff," I tell McKenna.

"I just wanted to get dressed," she says.

"Right. You can get dressed in my room. Just get your clothes from the closet and bring them over."

I hesitate a moment, then gather up her things from the bathroom counter.

Rachel is still describing the room to Don as I walk past, following McKenna to my room.

SIXTY

McKenna

Caleb sits in his bedroom while I shower and get dressed in his bathroom.

With the hot water running over my head, I focus on keeping my thoughts blank. It's the only way to control the random images that run through my head.

Silas Crowe watching me across the bar.

Silas Crowe watching me in the courtroom.

Jennie lying in a pool of her own blood.

Keeping my thoughts blank is the only way I can keep myself from shattering into a million pieces.

When I've calmed enough to not shatter, I think about

Caleb. About Don and Rachel. They brought me into their home. And this is what happens.

I shut off thoughts about Rachel and focus on Caleb.

I don't know what I'm supposed to do. I promised him I wouldn't just up and leave.

That request may have changed now. Silas Crowe has not only come into their shop, he has come into their home. With an obvious threat. Not to them, thankfully. But to me. A guest in their home.

As I dry my hair, I resign myself to having to leave here. If they want me out of their home, I'll go. No hard feelings. I wouldn't want me in my home. Not with threats like this hanging over me.

Dressed, I step out of the bathroom to find Caleb sitting on the sofa, waiting for me.

"Hey." He comes over and wraps his arms around me. "You better?"

"I'm okay."

"Bradley is here. He took photos."

"Good. I didn't intend to bring this into your home."

"You didn't bring anything."

"I did. I didn't mean to. But he followed me here."

"It's not your fault."

"Still. I can understand if you and Rachel want me out of here."

He links his arm with mine as we head out into the hall-way. "Didn't we just have this conversation? Rachel and I are here for you."

"It's too much to ask."

"And I don't remember you asking."

"Hello again, McKenna," Sheriff Bradley Winslow says.

"Hi." I push at my hair.

"I just got off the phone with the detective in Houston. He's on his way up here."

"So soon."

"We're taking this matter very seriously," Bradley says.

"Thank you."

"Do you mind if I ask you a couple of questions?"

"No. Of course not."

"Can we go downstairs?" he asks. "Sit down?"

Caleb takes my hand. "Let's go sit downstairs."

We sit on the sofa where someone, Rachel perhaps, already has a fire going.

"I want to ask you about the lipstick used to write the message," Bradley says.

"It belonged Jennie," I say flatly. I have no doubt about it. "She called it her signature color."

"Did you happen to bring her lipstick with you?"

"What? No. It would be with her things."

"Her things?"

"Her possessions. The police collected everything. After..."

"But you recognize it?"

I glance over at Caleb.

"She recognizes it Bradley."

"I just have to ask," he says. "It could make a difference

whether she has this lipstick with her or if he has it in his possession."

"He has it in his possession," I say quickly. "He must have taken it after he killed her."

"This will be important information for the detective to have."

"I understand that," I say.

"That's all I have for now," Sheriff Bradley says. "I'm going to leave you to get on with your morning. When the detective arrives, I'll send him here."

Sitting back, I stare into the flames. Caleb walks Bradley to the door where a steady rain is falling. I hadn't even known it was raining.

I realize this is a small town and I should have realized that the sheriff would have limited resources. I'm sure he's just doing the best he can do.

I let my mind go blank as I watch the mesmerizing flames.

A few minutes later, Caleb presses a mug of hot coffee into my hands.

"It's not coffee shop quality, but maybe it'll do for now," he says.

"It's good," I say. "Thank you."

"You should probably taste it before you decide."

I take a sip. "It's good, Caleb. You're very kind."

He takes a sip of his own coffee. "You're welcome. I feel like I should apologize for Bradley."

"He's just doing his job. I doubt he's ever had anything like this happen before on his watch."

"I'm sure he has not."

"Where are Rachel and Don?" I'd heard them come downstairs while Bradley was here, but I don't hear them now.

"They drove out to Don's house to get some of his things so he can stay for awhile."

I close my eyes. "I hate putting people out like this."

"Again. You didn't do it."

"Right. But if I weren't here, it wouldn't be happening."

"Not your fault," he says.

"You keep saying that, I might start to believe it."

"We can only hope." He smiles.

I smile back. "Thank you," I say. "For being so understanding."

"You and I have a deal. I'm understanding and you don't run off."

"You know. Eyewitness accounts have been proven to be practically useless."

"Are you saying there's something off with my memory?"

"Yes."

"Well. I'm merely adapting my memory to fit how it needs it to be for the current circumstances."

"That's usually an unconscious process."

"In my case, it happens to be conscious."

"What do we do now?" I ask, looking at him.

His blue eyes latch onto mine. "I don't know. I was hoping you would know."

"Then we're in a world of hurt, aren't we?"

"I think we'll figure it out. I do know one thing."

"What's that?"

"We aren't going flying today."

"No. I don't suppose we are."

There's the rain. And then there's the detective on his way in from Houston.

SIXTY-ONE

Caleb

Sheriff Bradley Winslow recommended I wait for the detective from Houston before I go into the attic. Just in case it's somehow related to the threat written on the mirror. I'm okay with that. I don't care for going up there anyway. Call me whatever you want, I'm more than happy to wait for the detective.

With nothing better to do, after breakfast, we open up the store and get to work on our lessons.

Today I teach McKenna about cook stoves.

When the door chimes, both of us look up sharply.

It's the local fly tyer, Richard, bringing in a box of new ties.

Richard is a middle-aged retired professor who is living his dream. A cabin on the river. No one to bother him, spending his days doing whatever he wants, coming into town whenever he wants.

"Richard, this is McKenna," I say.

"Oh. Good. Rachel finally broke down and hired some help."

"Not exactly. McKenna is my girlfriend. I'm just teaching her about the business."

"Even better," Richard says. "Welcome to the family. The Lawsons are good people."

"Thank you. I can see that." McKenna doesn't so much as flinch, but I have no doubt she'll have something to say after he leaves after me introducing her as my girlfriend. "I can see why people buy your flies for souvenirs. They're very well crafted."

"Yeah." He runs a hand through his beard. "They weren't supposed to be souvenirs. I made them to catch fish with. But I guess a sale is a sale."

"That's how I'd look at it," she says. "That and your art is out there in the world. Forever."

"You've got yourself a good one here," Richard tells me. "Hold onto her."

"I plan to."

"I've got to do some more errands, then get back to my cabin. My old dog is waiting for me."

"Good to see you, Richard. Come by anytime. Even if you don't have any flies to bring us."

"Thanks for the offer," Richard says. "Until next time."

He heads out, the bell over the door ringing behind him."

"He's an interesting fellow," McKenna says, watching him get in his truck and drive off.

"He is. Something of a recluse. But I think he just enjoys his solitude."

"Something to be said for that," McKenna says.

"Can be."

"He doesn't have a wife."

"I think he did. I'm not sure what happened there."

"I hate that for him."

"He doesn't seem lonely."

"Tell me about this stove," she says, changing the subject.

"Okay," I pull the cookstove she points to off the shelf and haul it to the counter so I can take it out of the box. It's so much easier to explain how things work when I can show her.

I glance at her as I work. Maybe she didn't hear me call her my girlfriend. Maybe she missed that comment. Thinking about something else.

She's got a lot going on right now. I lot of things she's got to process in her head.

I show her how to hook up the stove.

"If you were going camping, which stove would you take with you?" she asks.

"Probably this one."

"Why?"

"I just like the way it looks. The way it handles."

"Hmm. It seems sturdy, too."

"Are you thinking you'd like to go camping?"

"I'm thinking nothing of the sort. You can go ahead."

"I haven't been camping in years. The closest thing to camping I care about anymore is a walk down to the river."

"What made you lose interest?" she asks as we work together to pack the stove back up and put it back in the box.

"I don't know. Living in the city. I just got away from it."

"You like flying now."

"I like flying now. Yes. And you've never been camping?"

"I've never been outside of Houston until I started driving here."

"I find that so hard to comprehend."

"Houston's a big place. And it's got everything. Including parks if a person needs to get outdoors."

"I doubt it has fly fishing."

"I doubt that, too."

"I'll be right back," Caleb says heading to the back after putting the stove back on the shelf.

"Okay. I'll be here." I busy myself with straightening a display of t-shirts.

The door opens again and I only jump a little this time. A young couple wearing shorts and hiking boots steps inside. They look exactly like the kind of people who would go camping.

"Good morning," I say. "Welcome to the Outpost. Can I help you find something?"

"We're just looking around," the young lady says.

"We're about to go on our first mountain climbing expedition. Do you know anything about climbing gear?"

"Oh." That is not something I would want to steer anyone wrong on. Too much could go wrong.

Caleb comes out of the back. "They're going climbing," I tell him.

"Fun," he says.

"My boyfriend's the one who can help you with this," I tell them, walking away.

Caleb casts a smile in my direction before turning back to the customers.

"Where are you going climbing?" he asks.

CHAPTER
SIXTY-TWO

McKenna

I sit on one of the stools behind the counter while Caleb helps the young couple with their mountain climbing supplies.

He seems to know what he's talking about as he explains different ropes and safety gear. I wonder if he's ever been climbing.

Probably. Just because he doesn't like to go camping now doesn't mean he didn't used to do outdoor things. Being a pilot, he has the personality for things that create adrenalin rushes. A bit of a stereotype, but when the shoe fits...

They take their time. They seem to be enjoying the

process of preparing for their climb in and of itself. No doubt part of the experience.

I enjoy having a few minutes to sit quietly by myself.

I haven't had any time alone with my thoughts since I'd walked into the guest room and found a threatening note scrawled in Jennie's lipstick across the bathroom mirror.

The sheriff is probably skeptical that I would know that it was my friend's lipstick. Rightly so. It seems a bit far-fetched. Maybe if I had the lipstick with me it would seem more believable. Surely he doesn't think I wrote the note. I would have no motive for writing a message like that on the mirror.

If I don't have the lipstick with me, that means that someone, in this case Silas Crowe, brought the lipstick with him. That implies all sort of premeditation. For someone to have stolen the lipstick to begin with. Bring it across the country and write a threatening message for me to see.

That's a whole lot of not just hatred, but a whole lot of premeditation.

More than most people would have the patience for.

I have a feeling Silas Crowe learned patience during his trial. He sat there like a spider watching me. Planning all sorts of things. Planning his escape. Planning how he was going to make my life hell. And apparently planning ways to end my life without even knowing details about just how he would go about it.

An evil man, that one.

And he found me.

He not only found me, he got into the Lawson's house. In and out without being detected.

Just like he'd done at my condo.

He'd pulled it off again.

I keep thinking how close I came. I have no doubt that Silas would have killed me if he'd found me alone in the guest room.

Caleb saved my life by having me stay in his room.

I'm having a hard time wrapping my head around that.

Caleb saved my life and I'll be forever indebted to him for that.

The problem is that we aren't safe. None of us.

If Silas Crowe got into the house, which he obviously did, he'll do it again. He got into the house. Knew which room I'm staying in.

He knows too much.

I don't understand how he knows so much.

And at this point, leaving here won't help. Even without me here, Caleb and Rachel are still in danger. I wasn't there when he killed Jennie. He'll go after anyone associated with me.

Watching Caleb, I have that same feeling of helplessness come over me that I have whenever I think about Jennie.

But Caleb isn't Jennie and we're ready for Silas now. We know he's here and we know what he's capable of.

I refuse to let him stop me from living. I refuse to give him that power.

SIXTY-THREE

CALEB

I GET a message from Bradley letting me know that the detective from Houston is flying in and will be here around three o'clock. I'm just glad they didn't ask me to go pick him up. I would have had to tell them no.

I'm not letting McKenna out of my sight. Not only that, I'm keeping one eye on Rachel.

She and Don made it back from his house and got him settled into Rachel's room. She has a sofa in her room that he can sleep on.

Having sofas in the bedrooms is a perk of living in a big old house. I'll probably set up a twin bed in there sometime today, but there's no rush. Don is adaptable, like me.

At any rate, the thought of leaving McKenna and Rachel here while I'm off flying somewhere is not even an option as far as I'm concerned. So it's good that they didn't ask.

Just before Noon, the rain lets up.

"Let's close up the shop and walk down to the Hungry Biscuit," I say as I come out of the storage room after breaking down the last of the delivery boxes that came in yesterday.

"We don't usually close for lunch," Rachel says. She's sitting at her desk working on her computer. Don on the other side of the desk, doing something on his laptop.

"We don't usually have threats against us either."

"Good point. Don?"

"Sounds like a good idea to me," Don says. "I think we should all stay together anyway."

I clap Don on the shoulder. "You and I think alike, my man."

"Where's McKenna?" Don asks.

"She's behind the counter," Rachel says, glancing at the monitor. "Sorting that new supply of sweatshirts we just got in. She's doing a good job on the display."

"She's a good match for you, Caleb," Don says, looking right at me with his unfocused eyes.

"They haven't set a date yet," Rachel says off-handedly.

"I know," Don says. "He would have told me. As his best man, I would need to be informed so I can put it on my schedule."

I roll my eyes. "There's something wrong with the both of you. Talk about a good match."

Don reaches out for Rachel's hand. "Your brother thinks we're a good match."

"It took him a while to catch up, didn't it?"

"Nah. He's always known it. Everyone knows it."

"How do they know it, Don?" Rachel asks.

"People tend to know things that are true."

They smile at each other.

"I have to get out of here. I'll be out there with my own match."

Their laughter follows along behind me as I go into the shop where McKenna is.

"They sound happy," McKenna says, folding a red sweatshirt with an embroidered mountain scene on it and the words *Alpine Falls*.

"Yeah. It's ridiculous."

"It's sweet."

I pull up a stool and sit next to her.

"How are you doing?"

"I'm just folding these sweatshirts," she says.

"No. Really." I put a hand over hers. "I'm asking how you're really doing."

"I'm okay."

"Finding that note on the mirror was a lot."

She takes a deep ragged breath and meets my gaze. "Yes. It was. I honestly don't feel safe. I don't feel safe for myself. For you. For Rachel. For Don. And I don't know what to do about it."

Standing up, I pull her into my arms.

"I won't let anything happen to you," I say. "And Don feels the same way about Rachel."

"I know." Her voice is muffled against my chest. "But I don't think you understand how dangerous that man is."

"I think I do have an idea." I know that he killed her best friend. Doesn't get much more dangerous than that. "We're all watching out for each other. We know he's here. We know what he looks like. The sheriff has a photo of him from the video footage and he's sending it to all the merchants. He can't check into any place, the lodge, anywhere, without being detected."

"He could change his appearance again." she says.

"He can do whatever he wants to do, but he won't get past us. Okay?" I run a hand lightly along her back. "When the detective gets here, he'll work with the sheriff and they'll figure out how to catch him."

"I like your optimism," she says.

She doesn't believe me. I can tell she doesn't believe me.

She has every right to be skeptical about anyone's ability to catch Silas Crowe.

The man killed her friend. Tracked McKenna to Alpine Falls. Got into our house undetected. He has skills. No one is doubting that.

"I still feel like I should leave. I feel like I'm putting you in danger. But I know I waited too long to do that. He knows we're close and even if I left, he'd still use that against me. He would delight in hurting you. Maybe all of you."

"I'm just glad you aren't out there by yourself. I'm glad you found your way to us."

"You say that now," she says. "I just hope you don't regret it later."

"I understand," I say, kissing the top of her head. "I really do understand. But you have to accept that too many of us are looking for him now. Watching for him. He's going to get caught."

"I hope you're right. You don't know how much I hope you're right."

I hear Rachel and Don coming our way.

"We're going to walk down to the Hungry Biscuit. Get some lunch."

"Good idea. It's important that we stay together."

"I could get used to this," I say.

She leans back and looks into my eyes. Her teal green eyes sparkle.

"Come on you two love birds. Let's beat the lunch crowd," Rachel says, her arm looped with Don's. Nester walks along on the other side of him.

"Don's got it made," I say.

"Just hold McKenna's hand and quit complaining," Rachel says.

I send her one of those looks only a brother and sister would understand.

I like seeing her happy. It's been too long since I've seen happiness on her.

And no matter what McKenna might think, I'll always believe that in a roundabout way, she played a part in getting Rachel here.

McKenna

The detective, a man by the name of Henry Harrison sits on the sofa across from us. Anytime I've ever talked to him, he's always seemed distracted.

Conversations with him feel disjointed. I think it's because he doesn't bother with transitions. His thoughts jump around and his conversations reflect that.

And yet, despite that, maybe because of that, he's a good detective.

He already talked to Rachel and he went up in the attic by himself. Said he didn't find anything out of the ordinary.

"We never found her lipstick," he says.

"How did you know it was missing?" I ask, looking sharply at him.

"I'm sure you don't remember, but I asked you about it. That night."

"I don't remember that."

"You had lipstick on your hand. The same lipstick that was smeared across Jennie's cheek."

I look down at my hands. Unfortunately, all I can see is blood. The blood I had on my hands that night overshadows everything else.

It's what I see when I think about that night. Blood.

In an odd way, it's my mind's way of protecting me. I don't even see Jennie. Just blood.

Looking up, I meet Detective Henry's gaze. "Then you believe me? That the note was written in Jennie's lipstick?"

"I do. I know you would recognize it. And it's the same as what was at the crime scene in Houston."

"This is good, right?"

"It tells me that we've found our man. There's something else."

"What's that?"

He hesitates. I've never known him to hesitate before.

I glance over at Caleb who's taking in every word of the conversation.

"It's about Miles."

"What about Miles?" My heart slams into my throat. Not Miles. "Has something happened to Miles?"

"No. It's not that. Miles is the one who got him out of prison."

"How? Why?"

"I don't know. I just know that Miles has been working on the case. He's the one who found the technicality that got Silas out of prison."

I lower my head, letting the news spill over me.

Caleb puts a hand lightly on my back.

I take a deep breath. Let it out slowly. I'll have to think about this later. Now isn't the time to try to sort this out.

"Thank you for telling me," I tell Detective Henry, looking up to find him watching me with compassion. I can't see why he told me right now about Miles, but it's something I needed to know. I'm not sure about the relevance yet, but I'm sure I'll figure it out soon enough.

"What do we do now?" I ask him.

"You let us do our job. And." He looks at Caleb. "Keep each other safe. I suggest you use the buddy system. Nobody goes anywhere alone until we have Silas Crowe behind bars."

"Okay." I give him a little nod.

He's looking at Caleb again. "I don't want anyone minimizing the threat posed by this man."

"You don't have to worry about that." Caleb drapes his arm around me and pulls me close. Kisses the top of my head. "I won't let her out of my sight."

"Good," Detective Henry says. "I'm going to hold you to

that. I met Don and Rachel earlier before I went up in the attic. Do they understand the danger?"

"I think they do."

"Well," he says, standing up. "I'm going to swing by the store. Go over it with them one more time. I don't want anyone getting hurt."

"Thank you for coming up here, Detective," I say. "You've gone above and beyond."

"I just want to catch this killer. Put him back where he belongs."

"Under the rock he crawled out from under," Caleb murmurs.

Detective Henry grins. I don't think I've ever seen him smile before. It's a little disconcerting.

"Do you have a gun, Caleb?" Henry asks.

"I have one in the safe. Rachel keeps one behind the counter in the shop."

"Get your gun out of the safe. This is one of those times when you need it where you can get to it. No point in having the thing if you can't get your hands on it."

"I'll get it out," Caleb says.

"Thanks for your time. You have my number. Any time. Day or night."

Caleb walks the detective to the door.

I sit on the sofa and wonder why I don't feel any better. I'd halfway expected to feel better when he got here. But nothing is different. Silas Crowe is still out there. He's still a threat. To all of us.

Maybe I'm just tired.

Maybe I'll go to bed early tonight. Get some sleep.

A bath. I've been promising myself I'd take a bath. A relaxing bath and an early night seems just the thing for tonight.

Perhaps things will look better in the morning.

"Seems like a good detective," Caleb says coming back to sit next to me after letting Henry out.

"He is. Very dedicated. Do you mind if I borrow your bathroom? I'm thinking I'm going to take a bath and go to sleep early. I need a good reset."

"I think that's a fine idea. Take your time. I'll stay out of your way and I'll try not to wake you when I go to bed."

"Thanks." I start to walk off, toward the stairs, but stop and put my arms around him. "Thank you," I say.

"You don't have to thank me."

"I know. But I just want you to know that I'm glad I'm here and not out there somewhere by myself."

"I'm glad, too, sweetness. I wouldn't have it any other way."

Even though I believe his sincerity, I just hope he doesn't come to regret it.

It's a feeling I have every justification to feel.

It happened to me once.

I lost someone I cared about once.

I don't want it to ever happen again.

SIXTY-FIVE

CALEB

WHILE MCKENNA IS RELAXING in the bathtub, a much deserved respite, I use the time to do a few things.

I bring a twin bed out of storage and set it up in Rachel's room. Go ahead and put sheets on it. A blanket. Can't expect to ask a blind man to make up his bed. Not when his job is protecting my sister.

I put on a load of laundry and straighten up my room.

It gets dark early as it always does in this high part of the mountains. Once the sun drops below the mountain tops, it gets dark and gets cold.

Since we didn't do it today, we'll go tomorrow and get McKenna a new cell phone. I may have to start making a list. No judgements on making a list. I have a preflight checklist and a post-flight checklist I use with every flight. Keeps things from being overlooked.

Simple things that can be important.

McKenna having a cell phone could be important.

I open up the safe in Rachel's bedroom. The safe is in there because it's the largest bedroom, the primary. I can't remember the last time I fired a gun. I take a few minutes to clean it up, then put it in the drawer of the nightstand since it doesn't seem right leaving it laying around.

They always say that a gun left lying around is like handing it to a criminal.

I toss my clothes in the dryer, then head back into the bedroom.

Seems a bit silly, but I take my vow to keep McKenna in my sights seriously. Can't see her while she's in the bathroom, of course, but I can hear her. She's already out of the bathtub. I know because she's running the hairdryer. A comforting, normal sound.

I pull off my boots and take them into the closet to put them away.

Turning, coming out of the closet, I freeze.

Someone is standing in my bedroom.

I blink.

It's Silas Crowe.

"How did you get in here?"

Silas smirks. "Wouldn't you like to know?"

"I would like to know," I say. "What are you doing in my house? In my room?"

The hairdryer is still going.

My throat is suddenly dry.

Just because the hairdryer is running doesn't mean that McKenna is using it. The hairdryer could be lying on the floor, making it sound like McKenna is drying her hair.

I try to do a quick mental calculation. To figure out just how long she's been drying her hair.

I don't know her well enough to know how long she usually takes, so it's an exercise in futility at the outset.

Something, a panel, in the ceiling shifts and I look up. It's one of those aha moments. When a lightbulb of clarity suddenly goes off in my head.

He came in through the attic. Dropped into my room through the ceiling. It's an old house. Each room has access panels.

It's how he got into the guest room and how he got into my room just now.

"Figured it out, didn't you?" he asks with a sneer. "People aren't very smart. It's so easy to outthink people."

"You're right," I say. "People aren't very smart. But you." I give him a quick nod. "You're a smart man."

He grins a feral grin.

I just need to tell him what he needs to hear until I can get him out of here. Get him as far away from McKenna as possible.

Unfortunately, he's standing between me and the

nightstand. The detective was right about the gun being worthless if I can't get my hands on it.

I strain to hear any sounds coming from the bathroom besides the steady roar of the hairdryer.

"She's safe for now," he says, reading my mind. Then his eyes go dark. "I'm going to make you watch. Make you watch while I fuck the bitch. Then watch while I slit her throat. But don't worry. You won't live long enough to fret about it."

Like hell.

I stretch to my full height. Hold my arms out. Just as I would if I encountered a bear in the woods.

"I don't think you want to do that," I say, then add a bluff for good measure. "You're being recorded. And the police know you're here."

"Police don't scare me. Police are the dumbest of the dumb. Dumber than you and your sister cavorting with that blind man." He scoffs. "Like he can do anything."

I take a step around him, toward the bathroom, preparing to position myself between him and McKenna.

"Wasting your energy," he says.

"You're the one wasting your time. You could be doing something productive."

Apparently that was the wrong thing to say to Silas. He snarls. "You think I should be working in a store. Like you. Talk about a waste of time."

Good. He doesn't know I'm a helicopter pilot. So he doesn't know everything. This is encouraging.

"You're right," I say. It's much more productive to spend your days stalking and torturing and killing people.

The hairdryer stops and I feel relief and fear coil through me at the same time.

I clamp my mouth closed to keep from calling out to McKenna. She's safer in the bathroom. The longer she stays in there, the safer she is.

I take another step in the direction of the bathroom door.

Silas grins that feral grin again and I watch him in what feels like slow motion as he pulls a stun gun out of his pocket and points it at me.

"What are you doing?"

"You might recall what I told you. You're going to watch."

I hold up a hand as though to protect myself, but, of course, it doesn't work.

I feel the sting of the stun gun as it slams into my shoulder.

Good God. It feels like I just got stung by a thousand and one hornets.

It takes me to my knees.

Doesn't matter how hard I try to stay on my feet. Can't do it. I slide to the floor, landing in a sitting position against the wall.

My vision is blurry, but I fight against it. I fight to keep my gaze focused on him.

I try moving my lips to cry out. To warn McKenna, but nothing comes out. I'm paralyzed.

Silas stalks toward me, a rope in his hands. He's going to tie me up.

"Don't like this, do you?" he asks. Up close I can see that his teeth are yellow and his breath smells foul.

But I can't even flinch.

The bathroom door opens and McKenna steps out, wearing her pajamas.

Her eyes widen as she takes in the situation.

After a moment of hesitation, she darts to the door. Turns the knob, but it doesn't open.

"You have to wait your turn," Silas says to her.

McKenna tries the door again. Shoves against it. But it's somehow locked from the other side.

She bangs on it. Yells for help.

It won't do any good. Rachel and Don are still at the shop. They can't hear her. No one can.

The realization that she and I are going to die right here, right now, settles over me like a soft misty fog after a summer rain.

CHAPTER

SIXTY-SIX

McKenna

I turn off the hairdryer and, feeling relaxed, straighten up the bathroom before heading out to the bedroom.

I needed the hot, relaxing bath scented with lavender bubbles.

Looking forward to curling up with my book, I consider going downstairs to get a nice cup of hot tea, but I don't feel like interacting with anyone.

A quick check of the time tells me that Rachel and Don are probably still out at the shop. I don't know where Caleb is, but I don't think he'll be very far. Maybe downstairs watching television, taking some time for himself.

Feeling pleasantly flushed from the hot bath, I open the door to the cooler air of the bedroom.

It's quiet, no sounds from downstairs. No conversation. No television.

In fact, the door is closed. I can't remember if I closed it when I came up.

My gaze sweeps away from the closed door and snags. Any coherent thoughts leave my head.

Silas Crowe is kneeling on the floor, a sneer on his face and a rope in his hands. Caleb is leaning against the wall, his eyes glazed, his body not moving.

My first thought is to run to Caleb, but my second thought right the heels of my first, is to get help.

I dash to the door, but it's locked.

"You have to wait your turn," Silas says.

I try the door again. Shove against it. But it's somehow locked from the other side.

Banging on it, I yell for help.

No one hears.

No one is coming.

I turn and face Silas Crowe.

"What have you done?"

"Oh. He's just stunned." Silas shoves at Caleb. "Can't move. But he can watch." He grins an evil grin.

"Watch what?"

Instead of answering, Silas leans Caleb forward and begins the process of wrapping the rope around his wrists.

A weapon. I need a weapon.

I start for the bathroom to get my hairdryer. But I stop. Silas is bigger than I am. The hairdryer isn't going to protect me from him. Even if I could manage to get the cord around his throat, I have no delusions about him not overpowering me.

I need something else, but I don't even own a weapon of any kind.

But... I'm not in my room.

I'm in Caleb's room.

Don't guys keep knives and other things lying around that can be used as weapons?

I look over at Caleb. Stunned. He's just stunned.

There's no blood.

Not yet.

I force myself to take a deep breath. To stay focused.

But I need to stop Silas.

He's going make Caleb watch while he kills me. His evil plan is so obvious.

Then he's going to kill Caleb.

After that, he'll hide and wait for Don and Rachel. They'll be next.

He'll get all four of us on this one spree.

I've seen enough crime scene photos, read enough reports, prosecuted enough criminals to know how this is going down.

I don't have a cell phone to call for help.

We're locked in this room and we have no way to let anyone know.

If the door is locked from the outside, how did Silas get in here?

I shake off the questions. Doesn't matter right now. I don't have time right now to analyze the crime scene in progress.

What matters right now is finding a weapon. Guys keeps weapons in their rooms.

Caleb is shifting enough to make it hard for Silas to tie his hands behind his back.

Good man.

His room.

The nightstand.

I rush over to the nightstand and pull open the top drawer.

A gun.

There's a pistol lying there.

Caleb. Caleb got the gun out of the safe. Caleb did as Detective Henry suggested.

Love for Caleb spills over me, but I put those feelings aside for later and pick up the gun.

It feels heavy in my hand. Heavy and real.

I straighten and face Silas. Just as I hold up the gun, Silas gets to his feet.

He looks a bit baffled, but not deterred. He didn't expect this.

All the better.

But he's not going to let it stop him.

"What do you think you're going to do with that?" he asks.

"Turn around and put your hands in the air."

He just grins evilly. "You don't know how to use that. And if you did, you don't have the balls to do it."

He takes a step forward.

"You killed Jennie."

"That bitch was just sucking up good air. She deserved to die."

Using both hands to steady the gun, I level it toward him.

"Turn around," I say.

He doesn't turn around, but he doesn't come closer either.

"I went to prison because of you."

"You went to prison because you're a murderer."

He shrugs. "I don't kill anyone who doesn't deserve to die."

Caleb tries to say something, but I can't understand.

I look in his direction. He tries again, but I can't make it out.

Silas uses the distraction to step toward me again.

I see him moving out of the corner of my eye.

My gaze back on him, all I can see is the big hulk of a man moving steadily toward me.

The gun in my hands is still pointed in his direction.

Silas sneers.

And that's enough. It's all I need.

My eyes half closed, I squeeze the trigger.

The gun kicks and I stumble back, my ears ringing with the unexpected boom from the gunshot.

Stepping backwards, I pull the trigger again. Then a third time.

Silas is standing still now. A look of surprise on his face.

I'm certain I missed him, considering I've never fired a gun before. I was always going to get around to it. Getting to the gun range was just never convenient.

Now that lack of convenience is most unfortunate. No more putting off things for me.

I level the gun and prepare to make another shot, but Silas is falling. Not dramatically. Just falling. He just crumples onto the floor. And there's blood, pooling around him on the hardwood floors.

Dropping the gun, I rush toward Caleb. Wrapping him in my arms.

"You're okay," I say, hoping I'm right. "You're going to be okay."

Seconds later, the door opens and Rachel and Don come spilling inside.

SIXTY-SEVEN

CALEB

I SIT on the downstairs sofa, McKenna holding an icepack against my shoulder.

Other than feeling a bit dizzy, I feel recovered.

Henry is at the kitchen table talking with Rachel and Don.

They'd no more than gotten inside the house when they heard the gunshots.

"He got in through the ceiling," Don says. "Just dropped in through the attic access panel."

"How did Don figure that out?" I ask, taking McKenna's free hand.

"How does Don figure anything out?"

"That's a good point."

Henry comes and stands next to us. "You sure you don't want medical attention?" he asks me.

"I've got all the medical attention I can handle right here," I say, with a glance over at McKenna.

"Good. Well. I'm going to leave you be."

"Is everyone out now?" I ask, referring to the stream of police and medical staff who have been in and out of the house. They unceremoniously rolled Silas out of the house and carried his body off to Boulder.

"Everyone's out. We'll have follow up questions, but all is taken care of." He nods in McKenna's direction. "You did good."

"I don't know about that," she says wincing.

"Trust me. You averted a disaster. A quadruple murder if my gut is right."

"Mine too," she says.

"She saved our lives," I say, stating the obvious.

"Indeed she did. McKenna is the hero of the hour. I'll lock myself out."

"You're a hero," I tell her.

"I just did what I had to do."

"It's not supposed to go like this, you know."

"What do you mean?" She turns the ice pack over, sending a new chill down my shoulder.

"I'm supposed to be the one taking care of you."

"Chauvinist."

"Hardly. But isn't the guy supposed to save the girl?"

"I think you're trying to impose rules where there aren't any."

"You think? As an attorney, I would think you like rules."

"As an attorney, I like it when good prevails over evil."

"Everybody likes that." I stretch my shoulders and remove the ice pack. "I don't think I need this anymore right now."

"Trying to be a tough man."

"I think I've proven just how not tough I am."

She chuckles softly. "I think you handled being shot with a stun gun pretty well, all in all."

"You're very kind. But there's something else I've been wanting to do. Something I think I've put off long enough."

"You had an enlightened moment?"

"Something like that." Looking into her teal green eyes, I cup her cheek.

Her eyes flutter closed and she leans forward.

Yes. Most definitely been putting this off too long.

My lips touch hers and all the pieces of my life's puzzle come together.

I don't care if Rachel and Don were right from the very beginning about me wanting to marry her.

There's nothing I want more.

SIXTY-EIGHT

McKenna

Two Weeks Later

"It's Tabby," I say, frowning at my phone. Since getting a new phone with my old number, I've been getting lots of calls.

It's probably bad that I haven't spoken to Miles since I shot Silas Crowe... in self-defense... but I'm still trying to process why Miles was working on Silas's case behind my back. Trying to make sense of why he'd find a way to get Silas out of prison.

"You should talk to her," Caleb says.

We're outside taking our daily walk along a trail

following the river. Today we're heading up toward the falls. The Alpine Falls the little town was named after.

I think Caleb is trying to work up to taking me camping. Not going to happen.

"I know." I click answer and put her on speaker. "Hey Tabby."

"McKenna. It's so good to hear your voice."

"How are you?"

"I'm okay. But Miles is devastated."

"What is he devastated about?"

"About you refusing to talk to him and not coming back to work."

"Things are a little bit complicated."

"I get that, but he feels awful. You should talk to him."

We stop walking at the sight of an elk standing next to the river. The majestic elk twitches his ears, but he doesn't run.

"I will," I say, keeping my voice low so as not to frighten the elk. "When I'm ready."

Tabby doesn't say anything for a moment. "When are you coming back?"

I look over at Caleb. "That's undecided."

"You can't work toward being a judge if you don't come back," Tabby says.

"Dreams change," I say.

"Yours don't. You've always wanted to be a judge."

"Dreams do change, Tabby. And you know it. Tell Miles I'll call him one day when he least expects it."

"Okay," she says. "I'll tell him."

"Got to go. I'm right in the middle of something."

We disconnect the line and Caleb and I stand watching the elk.

"I'm think you have a mean streak," Caleb says.

"Why? Because I won't talk to Miles?"

"Because you're making the poor guy suffer."

"He almost got us all killed. I'm finding that hard to get past."

"True... but I think you came out ahead."

"How did I come out ahead?"

"You discovered that you like small-town life."

"True."

"And that people in a small-town need a good attorney."

"I'm learning that, too."

"Maybe even a judge."

"I hadn't thought about that."

"Don't lie to me, McKenna Lawson."

"You can't call me that." I look at him sideways with a little smile. "Yet."

"McKenna Monroe." He pauses for a beat. "Lawson."

I shove at his arm.

"You know it fits you."

"Maybe."

The elk must have heard us. He takes off running.

"All you have to do is stay," he says softly.

"All I need is a reason," I say, looking into his deep blue eyes.

"You know I'll give you a reason. I'll give you the moon if you want it." He takes both my hands and pulls me close.

"I don't need the moon, Caleb," I say, swallowing the lump in my throat. "I just need you."

"I'm all yours. I always have been. And I always will be.

Then he pulls me close and kisses me.

Out of the ashes of my life, I found everything I'd been looking for. Even what I hadn't known I'd been looking for.

EPILOGUE

The roar of the helicopter cuts through my headphones. I hold onto my seat as the helicopter tilts and pivots around a bank of white puffy clouds.

"What do you think?" Caleb asks, his voice sliding into my head with a smoothness that makes it sound like he's talking right into my ears.

"I think it's beautiful," I say. "The lodge down there looks like it's out of a storybook."

"Ready to see the town?" he asks.

"Sure." I'm belted in with a four-point restraint, but it doesn't feel like it. Since this is my first time in a helicopter, the lightness I feel is unexpected and not a little delightful.

Caleb pans the helicopter to the right and we go up in altitude again. I keep my head pressed against the window, not wanting to miss a single view.

Caleb keeps his eyes on not only the sky, but also the gauges. So many of them.

"Do you know what all of those are for?" I ask him.

"Most of them," he says, giving me a little smile.

"It must be a lot to keep up with."

"As long as nothing is beeping, we're okay."

"You sure know how to make a girl feel safe."

"You're safe and you know it."

I do know it. I'm safe with Caleb.

So much has changed in the last month.

He and I made a trip to Houston to pack up my condo and get it listed for sale.

I've made changes in my life I never saw coming.

And, yes, we had dinner with Tabby and Miles. Miles explained what happened that got Silas Crowe out of prison. The man's defense attorney presented some evidence that Miles couldn't refute.

From there things went from bad to worse until Silas was suddenly released from prison.

Me? I think I've had enough of prosecuting criminals for awhile, at least. I'm in the process of setting up a little family practice right here in Alpine Falls.

Miles is not happy that I'm not returning to Houston, but once he met Caleb, he understands a little better.

"Follow your heart," he told me as he hugged me goodbye after dinner.

And that's what I'm doing.

I'm following my heart.

"There's the Outpost," Caleb says, pointing below.

"And there's our house behind it. It's a really big house."

"Big enough to hold two full families," he says.

I look blankly at him.

"Unless you want us to get our own place. We can do that, too."

I smile a slow grin. We haven't talked about where we're going to live.

"I think Rachel and Don would miss us," I say. "Besides, I rather enjoy their company."

"Good." He squeezes my hand. "You know. Rachel's ready to set a date."

"They're getting married?" I knew they were going to. I just didn't know they were that close setting a date.

"It won't be long. They just want a quiet ceremony."

I turn my attention back to the window and bite my bottom lip.

So happy. Rachel is like a different person from when I first met her.

And I guess I'm a different person, too.

I'm not ready to spend the night in a tent, but I do enjoy our outdoor walks.

And, yes, dreams do change. Or maybe they don't change so much as they shift.

Being an attorney in Alpine Falls is a different experience from being a prosecutor in Houston.

I have time for a life outside of work and I find that to be utterly refreshing.

And maybe, just maybe becoming a judge is still in my reach for some day.

Maybe.

But for right now, I have other things are higher priority for me.

Like Caleb Lawson.

Like starting a family.

Like living my very own happily-ever-after.

Jennie would be so proud.

But I'm not doing it just to make Jennie proud... even though I like it that it would. I'm doing it because being with Caleb makes me happy.

I look over at him. So handsome. With his headset over his ears. His strong clean-shaven jaw. When he smiles at me, his whole face lights up and my heart trips and falls a little bit more.

Every time it happens, I wonder how I could keep falling more and more in love with him.

I didn't know it was possible for a person to be this happy.

What started off as a life in ashes has turned into a fairy tale ending.

And I, for one, could never ask for anything more than that.

. . .

The End.

Keep reading for a preview of
Borrowed Until Monday...

AUTHOR OF SECOND CHANCE KISSES
KATHRYN KALTECH
Borrowed
Until Monday
THE WORTHINGTONS

BORROWED UNTIL MONDAY

PREVIEW

Chapter 1

Hannah Adams

What I'm grateful for:
Even though things were bad, very bad, they
could have been much worse.
I'm grateful for not falling down.

Houston, Texas

Morning.

The break of dawn, to be exact.

At six thirty in the morning, before the world came back

to life after taking several hours to reset, was my favorite time of day.

Several hours for some people. For me, not so much.

Flipping on the light switch as I walked through the office door, I shrugged my oversized handbag off my shoulder and dropped it onto my desktop next to the closed notebook computer. Nothing else on the desk.

My name plaque was scheduled to be delivered Monday. Until then I was the nameless assistant to Jameson Beaufort, Vice President of Worthington Enterprises.

Considering that I had worked here for all of four days, counting today, and I had yet to meet Mr. Beaufort, today was going to be interesting.

Going around the desk, I sat in my office chair. I'd looked it up. It was one of those brands that cost more than a month's paycheck for me. But if a person had the money in their budget, it was more than worth it. I could sit in this office chair for hours with no discomfort whatsoever. It was a little like sitting on a porch swing.

If they ever needed an endorsement for their desk chairs by a real person, I was their girl.

I set one of those cardboard take-out trays from the coffee shop next to my handbag.

On one side was my own skinny latte—hot, on the other was a something called a cold brew. I had actually paid for cold coffee.

Never would have called that one.

I still had the text on my phone from Jameson Beaufort. Came in last night two minutes before ten o'clock.

MR. BEAUFORT

Starbucks. Trenta sweet cream cold
brew. Thanks.

As I had stood barefoot in my pajamas staring dumb-founded at the text message, another one had followed.

MR. BEAUFORT

Seven a.m. Use the company credit
card.

Sitting in my bed on the twenty-fourth floor of my studio apartment looking out over Uptown Houston, I had used my indomitable communication skills to interpret the message.

Mr. Beaufort, my new, as of yet unmet boss, would be in the office tomorrow at seven a.m. and he was requesting, using the term loosely, for me to bring him a coffee.

Yes sir.

Not just a coffee, but a big ass cold coffee. And since I didn't have a company credit card yet, I would be buying my new boss that big ass cold coffee.

I stared at the cold brew sitting on my desk and debated what to do with it.

Since it was already cold, it wasn't going to get colder.

Mine, on the other hand, would. I took a minute. Took a sip and closed my eyes. I'd almost forgotten how good a designer latte could be. And to think that only a couple of weeks ago, it was something I took for granted on a daily basis.

After a couple minutes debate, I decided that Mr. Beaufort would probably like to have the coffee waiting on his desk when he got here at seven.

Taking my time, I powered up my computer and logged in.

I'd been in Mr. Beaufort's office before. His mail was stacked neatly on one side of his desk where I placed it every day. I watered his ivy.

And I'd stood at the fourth-floor window overlooking the Skye Travels Airport private tarmac.

This particular building was only months old. According to what I had heard, Mr. Jameson still had his office downtown Houston but was in the process of moving up here permanently.

I'd learned quite a lot about Mr. Jameson from others in the breakroom one floor down.

He was something of an entrepreneur. If I had to guess, I'd say he had struggled to settle on a major. A pilot. The C-level officer of his own company. And probably other things I didn't know about yet.

The other assistants seemed to envy me my position. He was well liked. I could say that for Mr. Jameson.

I'd been hired by his grandfather, Noah Worthington,

mostly on my credentials and references. I was on a three-month probationary period. No harm. No foul. Probably why I didn't have a company credit card yet. The official reason anyway.

If I hadn't seen the tracking order forwarded to my new company email myself, I would have thought it was also why I didn't have a name plate for my desk.

No one had stopped by the office the whole time I'd been here. Either Mr. Jameson didn't have many visitors or everyone knew he was out for what was supposed to be the week.

But here it was Friday morning and he was on his way in.

Feeling a little nervous now, I took his coffee and headed to his office.

Like I had done a dozen times, I opened the door and stepped into his office. My office had a glass wall across the front with a view of the hallway, but early morning sunlight streamed across the wooden floor of his big floor to ceiling windows.

As I walked across the office toward his desk, a man wearing a business suit standing in front of the windows behind his desk turned around.

"Eek!"

I jumped, my feet, heels and all, literally left the floor and the ten-dollar iced coffee landed on the floor, spilling out in a flood of cream-colored liquid.

I was grateful that I hadn't twisted an ankle and landed sprawled across the floor myself.

"Mr. Jameson?" I asked, swallowing hard.

BORROWED UNTIL MONDAY

Chapter 2

James Beaufort

It was good to be back in Houston.

I'd been in Whiskey Springs for two weeks. Working with my cousins on a business venture.

Two weeks.

Whiskey Springs in the heart of the Rocky Mountains was nice, especially this time of year. In October the weather was cool in the day and cold at night, but the first snowfall hadn't fallen yet. Once it did, the weather could be unpredictable at best.

I liked it in the little town of Whiskey Springs well enough, but after the first few days, I started to miss good

Houston food. I was Houston born and bred. I'd always lived here and always would.

Before I'd flown up to Whiskey Springs, I'd been in the process of relocating my office from the River Oaks Worthington Enterprises building to the new Worthington Enterprises building at the airport.

If they'd had room I would have moved up here a long time ago since it was more convenient for me when I wanted to fly somewhere. Now that we had the new building, I'd staked out my office on the top floor. Had an unparalleled view of the tarmac.

My family was all about airplanes. My grandfather, Noah Worthington, had started Skye Travels with one airplane. And now he was a legend in the field of aviation.

He owned a fleet of airplanes from Cessnas to Phenoms. We jumped into airplanes like most people jumped into their cars. It was nothing for one of my many aunts and uncles or cousins and their wives to hop in a plane and fly somewhere for dinner or a play or shopping.

Young pilots fresh out of college vied to come to work for Skye Travels. Grandpa did all the hiring and he only hired the best.

We were a family business through and through with no apologies. Grandpa hired his own. But even so, we had to be good at what we did. No riding on his coattails.

Even though I was a Vice-President on the Board of Directors, I didn't work for Skye Travels. I had my own business. But, having Worthington blood via my mother, Ainsley Worthington Beaufort, I had all the perks.

While I was in Whiskey Springs this time, my grandfather had seen fit to hire a personal assistant for me.

I was on the fence about having a personal assistant. Never had one of my own. Skye Travels had plenty of staff running around for anything I might need.

I figured it couldn't hurt anything. Maybe it wouldn't be a bad thing.

I'd sent her a quick text last night asking her to pick up some coffee for me this morning. I had a meeting at eight o'clock and needed to be ready to go. Unfortunately, I was running low on very little sleep.

I heard her come in. Her name was Hannah Adams. But I didn't have the time right now to make small talk.

I'd been at my desk since four o'clock and almost had everything hammered out for the meeting.

I was taking a break, wondering if she had brought coffee with her, when she burst into my office without knocking.

She hadn't known I was there. In retrospect, I should have made my presence known. She'd doubtless gotten used to coming into my office while I was out. My mail was stacked neatly on one side of my desk and she'd watered my ivy.

"Eek."

She jumped when saw me and I stood there helplessly

watching as she jumped and my coffee dropped out of her hands and spilled across the floor.

"Mr. Jameson?" she asked as she somehow landed with her feet firmly back on the floor. I was impressed that she managed to stay upright.

We hadn't met, but I knew who she was.

What I hadn't known was that she was drop-dead gorgeous.

Long brunette hair secured at the back of her head with some kind of clips. A couple of long strands pulled loose on one side of her face. Whether by intent or accident, the effect was the same. Professionally sexy. Sexily professional?

Smooth white skin and beautifully big green eyes. And God help me, she was wearing glasses. There was nothing more sexy than a personal assistant in high heels and glasses.

She was wearing a skirt that hugged her like a glove, a white button-up shirt, and a cute little matching jacket, all in black.

She was absolutely stunning.

"I'll clean this up right away," she said, jarring me out of my daze. Despite her words, she stood looking helplessly at the mess. I could see the nerves all over her. It wasn't her job to clean this up and she knew it.

I calmly punched a button on my office phone.

"Betty? Would you send someone up with a mop?

"Right away, Sir."

I disconnected the line. "Someone will be right up to take care of it."

"I 'um." She looked from the me to the mess and back again. "I'll get you another coffee right away."

"It's not—" She turned and dashed from the room before I could finish the sentence. "necessary."

The break room coffee would do in a pinch.

Seconds later the front office door closed as she dashed out.

This was going to take a while. The nearest Starbucks was ten minutes away.

I sat in my chair and stared at the doorway.

This was nothing like what I had expected. Nothing at all.

Hannah Adams looked more like a sex goddess than a personal assistant.

This did not bode well for me.

BORROWED UNTIL MONDAY

PREVIEW

Chapter 3

Hannah

What I'm grateful for:
It's always good to have a backup plan.
I'm grateful for having a backup plan.

So much for first impressions. I had walked right into my new boss's office. Without so much as knocking. And dropped his trenta cold brew coffee sending it spewing across his floor.

In my defense, I had not known he was in.

Backing out of my parking spot in my 2016 Toyota Camry, I realized that I didn't know where the nearest coffee shop was.

I pulled back into my parking spot and checked my phone. It had to be Starbucks. He had been very specific.

My hands shook as I typed in the search. Ten minutes away. Ten minutes there. Ten minutes back. And ten minutes to get the coffee. This had cost me thirty minutes and another ten dollars.

Backing out again, I took a deep breath and squeezed the well-worn steering wheel. My parents had given me this car when I went away to college. It had been new then and had served me well. My family urged me to get a new car. Something that would be reliable. But this car had not broken down on me once.

And since I had situationally imposed practicality, I had no intention of adding debt to my already heavy student loans.

It was a good story. Very plausible.

Details mattered.

I needed to take a minute and clean the coffee splatters off my shoes.

Then I needed to figure how I was going to fix this worst possible first impression.

Could a first impression even be fixed? According to everything I knew, it was almost impossible.

But I had no choice.

Forty-five minutes later I pulled back into my parking space. Starbucks had been much more crowded this time of morning than an hour ago. Different location. Different time.

But I had the iced coffee.

As I waited for the elevator to open, I checked my watch three times.

Did this make me late for work?

It wasn't eight o'clock yet. I decided it didn't make me late since I didn't have to be at work until eight.

At any rate, I was a jumble of nerves.

My first three days of work had been so uneventful as to be boring. That was the difference, I decided as I rode up to the fourth floor.

Mr. Beaufort's office door was open. I went to the door, peeked inside.

He wasn't in his office and there was no sign of the mess on the floor.

I left the coffee cup on his desk.

As I sat down and logged into my computer, my nerves settled enough that my hands stopped shaking.

As Mr. Beaufort's personal assistant, I was pretty sure I was supposed to have access to his schedule.

Maybe it was one of those things he had to give me access to himself. In his own time. He hadn't even hired me. His grandfather had done that.

Mr. Worthington seemed like a nice man. An older fellow. I felt fortunate to have been interviewed by such a legendary man and even more so to be hired by him.

Things had been going so well. And then I had to go and spill his coffee all over the floor.

I put my shoulders back and continued the training

sessions I had to have finished by the end of the day. I had six more modules.

Today's first module was on ethics.

I had to pause the video three times before the first quiz.

My thoughts kept wandering back to Mr. Beaufort.

I'd only seen him for a brief moment, but it had been long enough for me to notice his tall, lean figure, his business suit. And his bold blue eyes that had watched me in bafflement.

He was a handsome man. No one had told me that he was handsome. I hadn't been prepared for that.

I was just finishing up the first module when Mr. Beaufort passed in front of my glass window looking out into the hallway and came straight into my office. Our office since his was behind mine.

"Hannah," he said, stopping in front of my desk.

"Mr. Beaufort." I got lost in his gaze for a moment before I remembered. "Your coffee is on your desk."

"You didn't have to replace it."

I looked down at my screen. Ethics. Go figure.

"I didn't make the best first impression."

He looked at me a moment with that same baffled expression he'd used when I'd spilled coffee all over his floor.

His grandfather had hired me and I had bungled the whole thing.

He was going to fire me.

"Come into my office."

Following him into his office, I was already trying to decide if I needed to call the employment agency or my aunt.

Not what I wanted to do. The process of starting over was daunting.

But a backup plan was a backup plan.

Keep Reading Borrowed Until Monday...
Get your copy at www.kathrynkaleigh.com
or any major retailer.

ALSO BY KATHRYN KALEIGH

CONTEMPORARY

The Gravity of Us Series

(Reading Order)

Just Breathe

Just Surface

Just Melt

Standalone Suspense

Out of Ashes

Alpine Falls (Maybe Yours) Series

(Reading Order)

Still Yours (Maybe)

Yours for Christmas (Maybe)

Forever Yours (Maybe)

(ALPINE FALLS)

Stranded in Alpine Falls

Belonging in Alpine Falls

The Spirit of Christmas in Alpine Falls

Christmas Wishes in Alpine Falls

Finding True North in Alpine Falls

A Ghost of Christmas Magic in Alpine Falls

Secrets and Second Chances

Honeymoon with a Stranger

Not Our Wedding

(SILVER PINES)

The Way Back to You

Back to Where We Began

When We Were Us

(ONCE UPON FOREVER)

My Forever Guy

Our Forever Love

Forever Vows

Finding Forever

Accidentally Forever

(TRUE NORTH)

Borrowed Until Monday

Still Mine

The Moon and the Stars at Christmas

Perfectly Mismatched

On the Way to Forever

A Merry Little Christmas

On the Way Home to Christmas

It was Always You

(UNBREAK MY HEART)

Begin Again

Love Again

Falling Again

(FOR THE LOVE OF THE FLIGHT)

Just Stay

Just Chance

Just Believe

Just Us

Just Once

Just Happened

Just Maybe

Just Pretend

Just Because

(MAGNETIC NORTH)

Second Chance Kisses

Second Chance Secrets

First Time Charm

Three Broken Rules

Second Chance Destiny

Unexpected Vows

(FALLING FOR CHRISTMAS)

The Heart of Christmas

The Magic of Christmas

In a One Horse Open Sleigh

A Secret Royal Christmas

An Old Fashioned Christmas

(CITY SKYLINE BILLIONAIRES)

Billionaire's Unexpected Landing

Billionaire's Accidental Girlfriend

Billionaire's Fallen Angel

Billionaire's Secret Crush

Billionaire's Barefoot Bride

(TRULY, MADLY, DEEPLY)

The Lady in the Red Dress

On the Edge of Chance

Sealed with a Kiss

Kiss Me at Midnight

The Heart Knows

(STOLEN ECHOES)

When Cupid's Arrow Strikes

Chasing Fireflies

A Chance Encounter

(EDGE OF THE HORIZON)

The Forever Equation

Pretend Boyfriend

All our Tomorrows

Kissing for Keeps

Out of the Blue

The Princess and the Playboy

(RED LIPSTICK KISSES)

Red Lipstick Kisses and Small Town Wishes

Stolen Dances and Big City Chances

Chance Connections and Upside Down Plans

A Christmas Kiss on the Twenty-Fifth

Believe in the Magic of Christmas

Vows of Inheritance Series

(Reading Order)

Vow to Protect

Vow to Redeem

ROMANTASY

(IN THE SPIRIT OF LOVE)

Spirits of the Heart

Out of Dreams and Ashes

Etched Upon the Heart

WESTERN ROMANCE

(LONE STAR HEARTS)

Wanted by a Texas Ranger

Saved by a Texas Ranger

(WHISKEY SPRINGS)

Finding Natalie

Promising Samantha

Falling for Allyson

Saving Savannah

Claiming Charlie

Rescuing Keira

Protecting Gabriella

Courting Isabella

TIME TRAVEL

(INTO THE MIST)

Written in the Wind

Scripted in the Stars

Destined in the Twilight

Promised in the Mist

Trapped in the Melody

(DRAGON'S BLOOD)

Dragon's Blood

Lavender Blue

Champagne Silver

Twilight Frost

Mountbatten Pink

(WHEN HEARTSTRINGS BECKON)

Rescued in Time

Meet me in 1879

(WHEN HEARTSTRINGS ECHO)

Messages Across Time

Falling Through to Forever

Once Upon a Winter's Spell

(BECKONED)

Before the Storm

Twist of Fate

When the Stars Align

Once Upon a Christmas

Once in a Blue Moon

A Wish Upon a Star

(BEGUILED)

When Lightning Strikes

Storm of Time

Midnight Storm

When the Moon Falls

Stormborn Angel

(SPELLED)

Time Tempest

The Heart Remembers

A Moment in Time

Moonlight Shadows

HISTORICAL

(TAPESTRY OF BLUE AND GRAY)

Shadows Beneath Magnolia Blooms

Secrets Among Southern Roses

(IT HAPPENED BY ACCIDENT)

Accidentally Alluring

Accidentally Married

(SOUTHERN BELLE CIVIL WAR)

Beyond Enemy Lines

Love Always

Hearts Under Siege

Hearts Under Fire

Away Down South in Dixie

The Reluctant Bride

Stay with Me

Jasmine Kisses

Magnolia Kisses

Gardenia Kisses

(THE QUINNS)

Wait for Me

Take Me Home

Keep Me Safe

FATED MATES

Riley's Mate

Aiden's Mate

Brayden's Mate

STANDALONE SUSPENSE

Lost and Found

All I Want for Christmas

Serenity

Courting Alley Cat

All of the books in each Series are standalone and can be read out of order. However, some books have characters from the previous stories in them.

Sign up for my NEWSLETTER to get all my romance releases, sales, Kickstarter announcements, and a **FREE** romance, SEALED WITH A KISS